COME MONDAY

Wild Irish, book 1

MARI CARR

PLAYLIST

Fans of Spotify! Now you can access the Wild Irish "titles" playlist.

Come Monday – Jimmy Buffett
   Ruby Tuesday – The Rolling Stones.
   Waiting for Wednesday – Lisa Loeb and Nine Stories.
   Sweet Thursday – Matt Costa
   Friday I'm in Love – The Cure
   Saturday Night Special – Lynard Skynard
   Any Given Sunday – Sandpeople

MONDAY'S CHILD

Monday's child is fair of face,
Tuesday's child is full of grace,
Wednesday's child is full of woe,
Thursday's child has far to go,
Friday's child is loving and giving,
Saturday's child works hard for a living,
But the child who is born on the Sabbath day,
Is bonny and blithe and good and gay.

~Traditional nursery rhyme

Keira Collins stared at the paper in her hands and bit back the growl of frustration that bubbled beneath the surface. She'd received another C-plus. Professor Wallace had finished handing out the graded work and was beginning his lesson on the importance of dialogue in fictional writing.

Screw him and his damn quotation marks.

She'd only taken this creative writing class on the advice of her advisor, who claimed she needed another English credit to fulfill the college's stupid general education requirements. So far she'd taken two years' worth of what she called "High School, the Sequel", all without setting foot in a single class in her major program. She wanted a degree in business technology, not to be the next freaking Nora Roberts.

The worst part of this class was, she knew her papers were perfect. English had always been one of her best classes in high school. She knew how to write a complete sentence—unlike Roy Decker. She glanced at the nineteen-year-old frat boy next to her to try to see what grade he'd gotten. She'd been paired up with Roy as critique partners the first week of class back in January. All that basically meant was she practically rewrote every word of his papers while he stared at hers and said, "This is real good."

Roy caught her gaze and flashed his paper toward her with an enormous grin, another C-minus, which apparently delighted the slack-ass boy to no end.

Great. They'd both gotten C's...again.

Her temper rose and she shot daggers at the back of her professor's head as he wrote the proper way to punctuate dialogue within a sentence on the white board. She'd tried—really tried—to use the man's asinine comments to improve with each paper, but it was clear she was beating her head against a brick wall—a six-foot-two-inch brick wall with light brown hair and soulful, deep brown eyes.

Crap, why did her teacher have to be so hot? He made her think completely inappropriate thoughts and she'd be damned if she became a cliché—the college coed who falls in love with her professor.

She'd refused to question Professor Wallace personally about her papers because the idea of being anywhere alone with him intimidated the hell out of her. When he looked at her, she felt as if he saw way more than just the surface and she was uncomfortable under his all-knowing gaze. Usually she kept her eyes averted as she took notes from the man's lectures lest she unwittingly reveal her less-than-scholarly interest in him.

But now it was mid-April, just two weeks from the end of the semester, and she'd finally hit her limit on all these damn C's. He was younger than most of her college professors—somewhere in his mid-thirties, she guessed, which should make him more approachable, not less. At twenty-seven, she was just old enough to feel completely out of place on campus as she watched the barely-out-of-their-teens student body discussing last weekend's wild parties. She should be old enough, mature enough to face Professor Wallace without babbling like a child. But there was something about the man. She didn't have trouble telling anyone what she thought and she considered herself a fairly independent, outspoken woman...with everyone except him.

He turned back toward the class and caught her eye. In the past, she would have scrambled to avoid that intense look. Instead, she narrowed her eyes and held his gaze. He stumbled momentarily over his words and she felt a small, petty smile curve the side of her lips.

She'd shaken Mr. Unshakable. Caused Mr. Perfect to lose his implacable cool.

He recovered quickly, finishing his thought, but his eyes refused to move from hers and she felt the moment stretching into a battle of wills. For several minutes, he continued to speak as if she were the only person in the room while she merely stared, not bothering to write down a word of his lecture. She'd pay for that stubbornness later, but right now the only thing that mattered was winning this war.

"Um, Professor Wallace." Roy's hand went up, forcing both of them to break their concentration.

"Yes, Mr. Decker."

"It's time for class to be over."

Professor Wallace grinned and Keira sucked in a deep breath at the sight. For a moment her confidence, her determination wavered and she considered avoiding the coming confrontation once again.

"So it is. I want you to bring rough drafts of a five-page

short story to class next time. There must be a lengthy dialogue included in the story. Class dismissed. Miss Collins," Professor Wallace added as she rose. "Please follow me to my office. I'd like to speak to you about your paper."

Shit. Double shit.

She'd gone too far apparently, tempted the bear from his den and he had taken the decision to discuss her grade out of her hands.

She stiffened her spine and watched the other students file out as she gathered her things. Once the room was empty, the professor gestured for her to precede him down the hall. She knew where his office was, having stood outside the closed door on more than one occasion debating whether or not to knock and question his grading practices. She'd never managed to work up the nerve. She was starting to think she wouldn't have held on to it tonight either.

They approached his office door and he unlocked it, again motioning for her to lead the way. As she entered the room, she heard the door close behind them.

She turned and glanced at the closed door. He followed her gaze.

"I want to ensure that we aren't disturbed." His words, though spoken lightly, sent a shiver of fear through her. His voice was deep, sensuous, and she found her thoughts drifting to places best left unexplored.

"How old are you, Miss Collins?" he asked.

She was taken aback by his unexpected question. "I'm twenty-seven. Why?"

"You're considerably older than the other students in the class." His reply was succinct, but far from an answer.

She didn't think it was any mystery that she was older than most of her classmates.

"I don't consider seven, eight years such a vast gap."

He grinned at her and again she felt overwhelmed by the power of his close proximity. Every time the man got within five feet of her, her body shifted into overdrive. Her nipples were erect, her breathing stilted, her stomach tied in knots.

"I agree. It isn't," he assured her, and she realized at that moment he wasn't completely unaffected by their nearness either. He seemed slightly nervous as well. "You don't live on campus, do you?"

As he spoke, his eyes covertly traveled down her body and she was struck by the fact that his wayward glance didn't bother her, as it did when patrons of the restaurant where she worked did the same. His look seemed to be more appraising, almost clinical, while with other men the look couldn't be called anything more than a leer, an unsavory study of her body. She'd long ago accepted that men found her pretty. With waist-length, wavy black hair, porcelain skin and ice blue eyes, she'd fought off more than her share of unwanted attention. Of course, it helped that she had four enormous, overprotective brothers at her back.

"No, I don't live on campus," she replied. She still lived at home with her father and siblings, still worked as a waitress at the family business, still did everything the same as she had when she was a teenager. She sighed as she considered his question and how dull her life truly was.

Her mother had passed away midway through her senior year and the raising of her six younger brothers and sisters had fallen to her. Not that her father had ever charged her with that duty. As the oldest, she'd simply assumed the role because, well, there hadn't been anyone else and because she loved her family almost to the exclusion of everything else. She wondered sometimes if she'd almost lost her own identity in that love.

She glanced at the clock that hung on his wall. Five

fifteen. She only had forty-five minutes to weave her way out of this unusual conversation and bust ass across town to be at work by six.

"You have some concerns about your grade, I believe." His astute comment, on the heels of his strange questions, left her reeling.

"Um, yes," she began, struggling to speak her mind under his intense gaze.

What would he look like without any clothes on?

That inappropriate question sent a flush of heat to her face and she watched his gaze narrow, his lips twitch slightly. He couldn't know what she was thinking. Could he?

"I don't understand why you keep giving me C's."

"I don't give grades, Miss Collins. My students earn them."

She rolled her eyes at the old teacher line and was surprised when her reaction provoked a light laugh from the man.

"I used to hate it when my teachers used that answer on me as well," he admitted.

"My papers are grammatically correct. I include paragraphs, proper punctuation and I know the spelling is flawless."

"And this, to you, indicates A work?" he asked.

"Yes." She looked up at him, wondering how they'd gotten so close. She could have sworn when they'd begun this conversation, he'd been halfway across the room. Had she moved? Had he?

"I've given you suggestions on every paper."

She scoffed. "The same suggestion on every paper and it doesn't make any sense. You say my writing lacks emotion. I've tried to address that, but you still say the same thing, every time. And you gave Roy Decker the same damn grade. His paper sucked."

"Miss Collins, this course is over in two weeks. Why are you only now questioning your grades? That comment?"

Frustration and weariness won out in her fight to maintain her anger. She still had an eight-hour shift to work. "I guess I thought I could figure it out on my own, but I can't. Fact is, I don't understand what you want from me."

He paused and for a moment she thought her question had taken him unaware, or somehow lowered his guard. "I want quite a lot from you actually."

She glanced at his face and was struck by the strange notion that his answer meant far more than schoolwork.

He must have recognized her confused look as he clarified, "I know what my students are capable of and I grade their work on an individual basis, on what I know they're able to produce. I'm sorry, but I won't discuss Roy's grade with you."

His laugh lines at the corners of his eyes crinkled as the beginning of his gorgeous grin peeked out again. She closed her eyes to block out the mouthwatering sight. She was fighting some serious arousal issues right now.

"I have high expectations of you because I know you are capable of writing something truly wonderful. There is more to writing than simply dotting the I's and crossing the T's."

"I understand that. I just don't know how to do what you're asking."

"Bring your papers—all of them—tomorrow. My first office hour starts at nine. Can you be here by then?"

She nodded. "Why?"

"We'll compromise. I'm going to show you what I mean about adding emotion to your writing and you're going to revise every paper, and then I'll re-grade them."

"We've written quite a few things," she said, trying not to have a nervous breakdown. Finals were approaching and the thought of rewriting nearly a dozen assignments made her want to cry. However, the idea of doing so much work paled in comparison to the thought of spending even more time alone with Professor Wallace.

"It may take us several meetings to get through all of them, Miss Collins."

"Keira," she said without thinking.

"Excuse me?"

"My name is Keira."

He nodded. "Keira."

Electricity shot through her body at the sound of her name spoken in his deep, sensual voice. For a moment, she envisioned herself tied spread-eagle to his bed as he whispered her name again.

Tied to his bed? What the hell kind of image was that? She blushed again as he took one step closer. She swallowed heavily when his gaze landed on her lips. Her tongue darted out to moisten them before she considered what her action might insinuate.

Was she inviting this? Him? To kiss her?

She struggled to breathe as they stood spellbound, motionless for one long moment.

He recovered first, clearing his throat and stepping away. "I'll see you tomorrow morning then."

She nodded, relieved—and oddly disappointed—to be granted so quick a reprieve. She turned toward the exit, ready to beat a hasty retreat.

"Oh and Keira," he said as she reached to open the door. She glanced over her shoulder at him. "Don't be late." His words were spoken lightly, but she sensed a darker, more thrilling underlying meaning. The words *or I'll punish you* hovered unspoken between them.

She held his gaze, nodded once and left.

❧

"YOU'RE LATE," TRISTAN CALLED OUT FROM BEHIND the bar.

"So fire me," she yelled back, glad there were at least some perks to working in the family business. She and her siblings could give each other hell for anything and everything at work, but all of them would still be employed in the morning.

"I was starting to worry about you, Kiki," her father said as he bustled out of the kitchen with a loaded tray in his hands. He gave her a quick buss on the cheek as he passed and she struggled not to roll her eyes at the pet nickname. She'd broken her siblings of using the annoying name years ago through sheer brute force and now they only used it in the midst of an argument because they knew how much the silly name irritated her.

"I'm sorry, Pop. Traffic was terrible. What are you doing carrying that heavy tray?" The doctor had issued a serious warning to her father regarding his high blood pressure in his last checkup and, as a result, she was determined to see him working less and resting more. The only reason she'd gotten him to the doctor at all was because he'd had a couple of dizzy spells. It had scared her to death so she'd sicced Teagan, her younger sister on him. Pop couldn't resist Teagan's puppy dog eyes or sweet, baby girl pleading.

To make matters worse, his high cholesterol was giving his off-the-charts blood pressure a run for its money, so the doctor had prescribed medication and a vacation. Unfortunately, telling Patrick Collins to relax was sort of like trying to convince the Pope to convert to Scientology.

"It's not heavy."

She fought back a groan of frustration. Damn man would work himself into an early grave. That thought, as always, scared the hell out of her and she dashed toward the stairs that led to their home above the restaurant. "Let me go throw on my uniform and I'll take over."

"Take your time. I've got things in hand here. The real dinner rush is only just starting," Pop answered, placing food in front of a couple of regulars before coming over to her with the empty tray in his hands.

"You're not supposed to be doing any lifting. Hell, you aren't supposed to be working at all. I thought we agreed that you'd take a couple of weeks off."

"Now don't you go lecturing me, Kiki. I'm older and wiser than you. That doctor is a flake, trying to get me to spend my hard-earned money on a bunch of useless pills." This argument was tedious in its redundancy. Patrick Collins was king of the conspiracy theorists, sure everyone from lawyers to doctors to pharmacists were secret government agents dead-set on taking his money.

He tapped his chest as he spoke and Keira sighed. "Who knows what this body can do? Me, that's who. This ticker has plenty more mileage on it."

Keira gave in, only because she was anxious to continue the fight in her uniform so at least she could be waiting on the tables and cutting down on some of her father's workload.

"Fine, Pop. You win for now. Let me go change and I'll help you."

As she climbed the stairs to the family's living quarters, she ran into Sean, her youngest brother, at the door. She loved all her siblings dearly but if forced to decide, she had to admit to a special fondness for the eighteen-year-old Sean. Perhaps it was because he felt more like her own child, rather than just a brother. While she'd merely taken on the mother role figuratively in her other siblings' lives, she truly had raised Sean, who had only been nine when their mother died.

"Where are you going?" she asked as he put on his coat. "It's a school night." Even as she asked the question, she internally winced. She just couldn't seem to kick the mother hen habit where he was concerned.

"Big history project due tomorrow. I'm going to Chad's house to work on it."

"Oh, okay. Well listen, don't be too late. Did you eat something?"

"Chad's mom's having lasagna. She invited me to eat with them."

"Sorry about dinner," she said, guilt pummeling her. Prior to her decision to attend college, she'd always made sure there was at least something on the table for dinner. Her mother had ensured the family gathered for dinner upstairs, away from the hubbub of the restaurant, and for years Keira had managed to maintain that tradition. In many ways, she felt as though she was letting her family down through her decision to continue her education.

Sean grinned and gave her a quick hug. "Are you kidding me? Chad's mom makes the world's greatest lasagna. She makes it from scratch."

She laughed. "What? You mean people actually eat lasagna that doesn't come in a box marked Stouffer's? You're kidding me."

"Riley would flip out to hear you even mention frozen lasagna."

Keira nodded. "Yeah well, that's clearly why she took over the cooking duties as soon as she was old enough." Riley was destined to become the greatest chef in Baltimore. Despite being only twenty-one, she was setting the city on its ear with her delicious recipes. Since she'd assumed the role as chef in the restaurant, business had nearly doubled as folks came from far and near to eat her traditional Irish dishes.

"I gotta go or I'll be late. See you later, Keira."

"Bye, Sean. Be careful." He rolled his eyes at her warning. It was the same warning she gave him every time he left the house. They were the identical words her mother had always said to *her* and she was determined Sean would have the same life he would have had if their mother hadn't been taken from him when he was so young.

She changed quickly and returned to the restaurant just in time for the dinner rush. She was so busy she didn't have time to worry about the prospect of returning to Professor Wallace's office until she fell into bed that night. It was well after two a.m. and she knew she should be too tired to think, but her mind kept lingering on a dangerous, delicious fantasy.

In her thoughts, she'd overslept and was running late...

She rushed into Professor Wallace's office shortly after nine with an apology hovering on her lips.

"Shut the door, Miss Collins," he said before she could speak. "And lock it."

She obeyed, wondering at his too-calm disposition.

"Come here."

Again she complied and a tiny part of her marveled at his ability to make her follow his commands. She wasn't the type of person to take orders easily from anyone. She'd spent far too much of her life in charge, the responsibility of caring for her family weighing heavily on her shoulders.

"You're late," he said.

Again she started to apologize, but he placed a firm finger against her lips, halting all sound.

"I warned you."

She nodded.

"Turn around and bend over the desk. Lift your skirt in the back."

She shivered at his request before her fantasy broke briefly.

Why am I wearing a skirt? I never wear them.

Shrugging off the wayward thought, she bent over his big desk, her mind only slightly aware of the fact the surface had been cleared.

His hand lightly brushed the back of her thigh as he helped her raise her skirt to her waist. She whimpered softly at the impact of his touch.

"Shh," he soothed. "This is for your own good." As he spoke, he brought his hand down against her buttocks. Over and over he spanked her as she trembled against the wooden desk. Her body revolted against her mind, the ingrained part of her that said this was wrong, as she lurched back, aching for more of his blows. His hand fell without restraint, without ceasing, and before she could make sense of what was happening, she came. Loudly.

"Ahh!" Keira bolted upright in bed and glanced around, afraid she'd woken her sisters with her cry. Riley and Teagan didn't stir, a fact for which she was grateful. They'd think she'd had a nightmare and there was no way she could explain *that* fantasy to them.

She silently gasped for breath, her body trembling, demanding the climax she'd dangled in front of it then ruthlessly denied. A trickle of sweat ran down her cheek. She wiped it away, wrapping her arms around her bent knees, trying to regain some semblance of control.

She'd never fantasized about such things before entering Professor Wallace's class. In the four short months she'd been his student, her mind had wandered to so many dark, forbidden places she wondered if the man had somehow hypnotized her. She'd never experienced such intense, powerful fantasies. She took a deep, calming breath and lay down again.

Figured. Her first real taste of hardcore, passionate need and it was directed at a man who was completely unattainable. He was her teacher, for God's sake. She glanced at the clock. In six hours she would be alone with him—and heaven help her, because she was sure she'd never be able to hide her desires from his too-knowledgeable gaze.

He was too perceptive, too attentive.

Too everything.

❧ 2 ❧

Keira stood outside the door to Professor Wallace's office and took a deep breath. It was five minutes to nine and she was functioning on less than two hours sleep. She'd tossed and turned most of the night, distracted by one red-hot fantasy after another. It seemed the good professor had hit three sevens in her sexual jackpot and had released the flood of coins—or in her case—unending, flowing arousal.

No use prolonging the agony. She straightened her bag on her shoulder and knocked.

"Come in," his deep voice beckoned. She shivered at the sound and wondered how in the hell she'd make it through this meeting without ripping her clothes off and throwing herself on his desk.

Opening the door, she stepped inside, tentatively hovering on the threshold. He looked up from the stack of papers before him and offered her that too-gorgeous smile.

"You're right on time, Keira. I like that."

She nodded and smiled tremulously. One glance at his

handsome face and her body was already staging its own show. A quick glance down proved her nipples were rock hard and poking through her cotton blouse. As she started across the room, she felt an unfamiliar stickiness between her legs. Christ. She was soaking wet.

"Please shut the door," he said, after she'd only gone two steps. She turned to close the door with a shaking hand and cursed her weakness. She was running on empty and seriously wishing she'd gotten some sleep.

As she approached the desk, she stopped and stared briefly at the smooth surface. For a moment, her dream of lying facedown upon it drifted back and she felt a rush of heat flush her cheeks. Mercifully, Professor Wallace didn't seem to notice her distress.

"I trust you brought your past assignments."

She nodded and reached into her bag, pulling out the endless stack of C papers she'd accumulated over the semester.

"I thought we'd begin by looking at the very first paper you wrote for my class again. I believe it was the one-page description of a special place."

She shifted through her essays, recalling her dismay at discovering a C-minus on her first paper. Little did she know the trend would continue for weeks on end. She'd been pleased with her description of the restaurant and sure the paper would receive an A. Finding it in the stack, she handed it to him.

"Ah yes. You wrote about your family's restaurant, Pat's Irish Pub. An interesting choice." He looked down as he spoke and she remained silent as he briefly skimmed her writing. "This is the family restaurant where you work."

She nodded. She'd yet to speak a word, too afraid her voice would betray her nervousness, her agitation.

"Tell me why you chose the restaurant as your special place."

She considered his question for a moment, wondering how much she should share. She shrugged. "I suppose I wrote about it because I've spent so much of my life there."

He frowned and she sensed he wasn't happy with her answer. "I've lived in the same apartment for twelve years. I wouldn't choose it as my special place merely because of its familiarity."

Twelve years. Again, she tried to guess his age. If he began teaching at twenty-two, he could be as young as thirty-four. He cleared his throat and she shook herself, aware he was waiting for her response.

"The restaurant is more than just a home to me." The moment he'd issued the assignment, she'd known she would write about the restaurant. It was the first place she'd thought of.

"What is your major, Keira?"

She sucked in a breath at her name on his lips. Why did the mere sound of it run through her like a tornado-force wind?

"I'm a business major."

"That makes sense," he replied with a nod.

"I don't understand."

He grinned. "In my experience, business majors tend to cut to the chase. They are rather no-nonsense kind of people."

She thought he'd described her well. She also knew he didn't consider his words to be a compliment.

"Your description of the restaurant is very factual, very observant, very boring."

She narrowed her eyes. "It's detailed and accurate."

"Close your eyes, Keira."

Her voice seized up as she considered his request. When she was able, she muttered one question. "Why?" Her heart raced at the idea of leaving herself even a tiny bit vulnerable in his presence.

"I want to do an experiment." He waited and she realized that refusal would be futile. Professor Wallace was a man who didn't take no for an answer. That thought sent a fresh round of juices to her already-drenched panties and she squeezed her legs together to fight the onslaught.

He quirked his eyebrow and she slowly closed her eyes.

"Describe this room." She started to open her eyes but he halted her. "With your eyes closed."

She struggled to remember what any part of the room looked like. She'd been so preoccupied with the office's lone inhabitant that she'd failed to truly look around. The only piece of furniture that seemed vaguely familiar was the desk, and even then, only from her rather raunchy fantasies.

"There's a desk in the middle of the room," she said at last.

His light chuckle sent her hackles up and she forced herself to try to think of more. "There are bookshelves on the wall." Which wall, she couldn't recall.

"Stop relying on what you can see, Keira."

She considered his suggestion and realized she could sense many things about the room. "It smells of leather in here. Leather and old books and," she paused, sniffing the delicate odors, "your cologne."

"Very good. What else?"

She turned her head slightly and was immediately struck by the silence. "I can't hear anything. It's remarkably quiet in here."

He seemed to agree. "One of the reasons I hold my office hours so early. I relish the peacefulness. By this afternoon, the noise of all the students out in the hallway and on the campus outside my window will fill this room. You mentioned the desk. It's right in front of you. Touch it."

She bent forward, thankful her eyes were closed, praying he couldn't detect the slight shaking of her hand.

"How does it feel?"

"Smooth," she replied, running her hand along the surface. "And cooler than I would have imagined. It would feel cold against my cheek." Her eyes flew open when she realized the strangeness of her remark.

Professor Wallace's eyes were studying her intently.

She cleared her throat, anxious to fill the uncomfortable silence with noise. "I, um, I see what you mean."

He nodded slowly and she wondered if he'd question her comment.

"Close your eyes again," he instructed. She complied, aware that the previous silence of the room was now filled with the unbearable loudness of her pounding heart. "Describe your family's restaurant. Don't tell me what you see, Keira. That's already in the paper. Tell me the rest. Tell me why this place is so special."

Thankful he hadn't questioned her observation about his desk, she envisioned the pub. "My family lives above the restaurant. I'm one of seven children so I suppose you can imagine it's pretty crowded. My mother was the cook before she died and on special holidays, when the restaurant was closed, she'd go downstairs to the big kitchen to prepare our meals and we'd eat at the tables in the big dining room. Even though the restaurant was basically home, my mother always made it feel like we'd gone out somewhere special to eat."

She paused for a moment, smiling as she recalled the extra effort her mother expended to ensure the holidays were always perfect for her children. The tablecloths, the candlelight, the grape juice served in fancy wineglasses that they all used to make toasts and laugh and pretend they were grown-ups.

Professor Wallace's next question brought her back to the present. "I imagine the restaurant must have smelled lovely."

She started to open her eyes to respond to his question but she realized that, without sight, there was a security, a safety in speaking her mind that didn't exist when she could see his face. If she was looking at him, she would fail to concentrate on her subject and instead spend too much time trying to figure out what he was thinking of her recollections. She kept her eyes firmly shut.

"The smells were incredible, warm and sweet. I know Christmas can't really have a smell, but in my mind, it does. Cinnamon, pine, fresh-baked bread."

"And your mother?" he asked.

Keira smiled. "She had a smell too. Sugar cookies. My mother smelled like sugar cookies." The memory, the brief burst of happiness at recalling her mother's scent, turned quickly to the piercing sadness that had resided in her heart for nine years.

"What about the sounds in the restaurant?" he asked.

She sensed he hoped to return her to the joy of the scene, but it was gone. She opened her eyes and looked at him as she spoke.

"My mother sang as she cooked. She had the most beautiful voice I'd ever heard. Well, except for Teagan, my sister—she has my mother's talent for singing."

"Look at your paper, Keira."

She glanced down at the page and briefly read her staid descriptions of the tables, chairs, bar. She'd spent nearly an entire paragraph describing the color and texture of the walls.

He tapped his finger on the paper. "The place on that

paper doesn't seem very special to me. The place you just described sounds like one of the nicest places on earth. Write about that place."

She looked up and nodded. "I understand."

He grinned and, for the first time, she returned it. "There were two other assignments," he picked up her stack of papers and flipped through it, "that would benefit from that same sort of description. Engage all your senses and rewrite these three papers. You can turn them in tomorrow morning when we meet again. Nine o'clock still okay?" He handed her the assignments and she mentally tried to figure out how in her busy schedule she was going to revise three assignments by tomorrow.

"Nine is fine."

"I'll see you tomorrow then," he said, and, dismissed, she turned to leave.

❧

AS THE DOOR CLOSED BEHIND HER, WILL SANK DOWN INTO his leather chair and tried to understand the grip this young woman had on him. He'd never been attracted to a student before, yet from the first moment she'd stepped foot in his class, Keira Collins had shaken his unwavering sense of self down to a pile of rubble. She'd destroyed his willpower and was systematically, unwittingly breaking down every standard, every principle he'd built his career upon.

Clasping his hands together, he wondered how in the hell he'd manage to keep his hands off her these next two weeks.

He'd been a damn fool to invite her to his office last night, and then outright insanity had claimed him as he'd extended the offer to work with her on her writing—alone, every morning. He was tempting fate in the worst possible way. He was a teacher and he could not—would not—seduce a student. The fact she was older and far more mature than his usual pupils shouldn't make a difference.

But Keira *was* different, very different. And in ways he suspected she didn't even realize herself.

He prided himself on his ability to keep his intensely personal life just that—personal. No doubt his colleagues at the college would be shocked to learn of his lifestyle off campus. A dominant lover, he worked damn hard to make sure the lines between his professional and personal life were kept clean, clear and distinct.

Keira was a true danger. He was walking a tightrope without a net and every step closer to her threatened to send him crashing to earth. He never approached women sexually outside his set of acquaintances because he knew there was no way someone untutored, unfamiliar with the practices of D/s could handle him in the bedroom. He confined his relationships to women who craved bondage, a strong hand, submission. He wasn't about to initiate a novice into that lifestyle.

Leaning his head back against his leather office chair, he closed his eyes and saw Keira's lovely face in his mind's eye. In his world she would be considered an innocent. Regardless of her past sexual experiences—and he suspected even those were limited—she wouldn't understand his need to tie her up, spank her, control her.

Or would she? Her constant blushes, her reluctance to return his gaze—always keeping her eyes averted—screamed of a submissive nature. Most telling had been her comment about his desk. Had she imagined herself leaning over it, her cheek pressed against the cool surface? The image of seeing her in such a position sent a surge of blood to his already full cock as he played the scene out in his mind.

He would command her to remove her pants—dammit, he hated jeans, and yet on her, the denim clung to her soft curves in such a way that made his fingers twitch at the thought of peeling the material off her.

Once she was bare from the waist down, he'd gently push her forward over his desk...

She gasped at the feeling of the cool wood against her delicate cheek.

"Do you want me?" he asked.

"God, yes," she hissed.

"I'm going to take you, Keira. Fuck you. Make you mine."

She moaned softly at his words, her palms pressing tightly against the desk. As he slowly entered her tight pussy, he slapped her lovely ass, surprised by her response. Pushing toward him, she silently begged for more as he bent over her back, covering her slight frame with his larger body. "I'm going to fuck you hard and you're going to come for me—several times. Do you understand?"

She nodded.

"Say it out loud, Keira. Tell me what you want."

"I want you to fuck me hard," she whispered. "Spank me."

Resting his head on her shoulder, he tried to process her request.

She would accept his spanking, his powerful thrusts, and he couldn't wait to introduce her to even more. How would she respond to bondage? He pushed his cock into her tight sheath.

"Yes," she whimpered as he began to thrust inside her faster, harder. The sound of his thighs pounding against hers as loud as—

The knocking on his office door recalled him to the present.

"Professor Wallace?"

Shit, he'd been a minute away from actually coming in his pants like a fifteen-year-old boy—from an inappropriate daydream about a student. He was in worse shape than he realized. He moved forward until the lower half of his body was concealed beneath his large desk.

"Yes," he called out.

Jennifer Smythe entered. "I was hoping I could talk to you about my courses for next semester."

He nodded, working overtime to resume his calm, cool advisor demeanor, forcing the fantasy of fucking Keira Collins out of his mind.

"Of course, Jennifer. Please come in. Have a seat."

It was going to be a damn long day. Hell, it was going to be a long two weeks.

"Keira, why don't you call it a night? You've been working your ass off the past couple of weeks and you look like dog shit."

"Thanks, Tris. Great compliment."

Tristan flashed his typical annoying brother smirk then poured a glass of merlot, setting it on the bar before the blonde who'd planted herself right under his nose earlier in the evening. The woman was working overtime to catch her brother's attention and, for some reason, he wasn't taking the bait. Keira had begun to wonder if Tristan wasn't interested in someone else. In the past, he'd been the ultimate womanizer, never passing up the chance to charm the pants off a lady, but lately she'd noticed he kept to himself. She sighed. Just one more thing she hadn't had time to think about since struggling through this semester's courses.

For the past two weeks she'd been living on virtually no sleep. Working at the restaurant, studying for finals, revising her English papers and fantasizing about Professor Wallace had sucked up every available second of her life. Her family had taken a backseat and the idea that she was letting too many things slide in regards to them was bugging the hell out of her.

In addition to Tristan's sudden disinterest in women, Sean's graduation from high school was coming up in a month and she'd yet to begin plans for a celebration. Her father was still working too hard and she wasn't even sure he was taking the medication the doctor had prescribed. Teagan had a nasty cold, which had curtailed her singing and put her out of sorts. Riley was going through some sort of bizarre *Hell's Kitchen* phase, pissing off all the kitchen assistants and causing them to quit, which was driving Ewan insane as he was in charge of hiring replacements.

The Collins siblings were heading toward a major blowup and Keira felt responsible for the heated tension hovering over the pub.

In the past, she'd been the counselor, the voice of reason, the calming influence. Since her decision to go to college, the past two years had cranked the treadmill of her life up to top speed and she felt helpless as she watched all the people she cared about getting tossed off the track.

"Earth to Keira." Tristan waved a hand in front of her face. "It's Thursday night and the place is dead. Joyce and I can take care of things. Go get some sleep."

She shrugged, aware that sleep wasn't something she seemed capable of anymore. She'd walked out of Professor Wallace's classroom for the last time yesterday and all she could hope was that eventually her intense fantasies about the man would die down. Until then, she seemed doomed to restless sleep that left her body aching and needy in ways she couldn't begin to understand or attempt to explain to her brother.

"Can I get you something to drink?" Tristan asked someone who had walked up to the bar.

"I was hoping perhaps this lovely woman could wait on me. Good evening, Keira."

She turned slowly, surprised to find the man tormenting her dreams standing behind her.

"Professor Wallace."

For two weeks, she'd reported to his office every morning at nine. During their sessions, he'd challenged her to express her feelings, her emotions in her writing. Used to playing her cards rather close to her chest, she'd struggled at first to reveal so many personal thoughts. As more time passed though, she'd found their sessions almost therapeutic—a fact that would probably annoy him to discover—as she talked about her concerns for her family, her difficulties dealing with her mother's death and her decision to pursue a college degree. With each session, she'd found her infatuation for the man growing and solidifying.

Why is he here?

Her mind raced over the possibility that perhaps her interest in him hadn't been one-sided. There had been just a few moments in his office when she'd thought his attention toward her had been more than that of pupil and teacher. He'd never made any improper advances, never said anything untoward, but sometimes she would catch a look on his face or he'd say something in a tone that made her think, made her hope that he liked her too.

Dear God, please let that be true.

"You're no longer my student, Keira. I think it would be perfectly fine for you to call me by my first name now. It's Will."

Her lips twitched. "William Wallace?"

He chuckled and acknowledged her joke. "Neither of my

parents finished high school. Unfortunately, I think they must have dropped out just prior to any mention of Scottish history. My mother's father's name was William and—for better or worse—I'm his namesake.

"Well, it's a very prestigious name. Let's hope you meet with a better end," she teased.

"Amen to that. I have to say the name was never much of a problem until Mel Gibson decided to make the movie *Braveheart*. It's been kind of downhill since then."

"Can I get you something to drink?" Tristan repeated, his tone a bit less friendly this time.

Keira glanced back at her brother, surprised to find him still hovering.

"I'd like a Guinness," Will replied.

"Um, Professor Wallace...I mean, Will. This is my brother Tristan. Tristan, this is my creative writing teacher from the college."

"Nice to meet you." Will extended his hand to shake her brother's. Tristan returned the gesture but Keira could see her younger sibling assessing the man's worth. She fought against rolling her eyes. At least Tristan's twin, Killian, was serving with the army in Iraq or she'd be dealing with identical bulldogs. She'd spent far too much of her life watching her brothers visually dissect and scare away potential dates. It seemed that in the eyes of her brothers, no man would ever be good enough for her. Tris was the worst; he seemed to assume all men wanted one thing and one thing only.

If he noticed Tristan's intense study, Will ignored it and turned back toward her. "I was hoping perhaps you could join me for a celebratory drink. Toast the end of the semester with me."

She nodded, taking off her apron. "As luck would have it, my shift just ended. I'll have a Guinness too, Tris."

Her brother narrowed his eyes but poured the two beers, placing them on the bar. Keira grinned at his attempts to keep her close and decided to throw a wrench into Tristan's plans. "Why don't we grab a table?" she suggested.

Will picked up the beers and led her away from the bar. She started toward one of the tables in the center of the room, but Will steered her instead to the corner booth. The idea of being in such a dark, isolated corner with him sent needy shivers of unease down her spine.

She'd resisted making a fool of herself in his office, managing to avoid flirting with him and—God forbid—making an outright play for him. She suspected now that he was no longer her teacher and they were on more even ground, it would be next to impossible to hide her undeniable attraction.

Placing the drinks on the table, he gestured for her to sit first. It was a circular booth and she'd expected him to sit down from the opposite side. When he followed her into the booth, she tried to ignore the fact that he'd planted himself right next to her, sitting far too close for her tenuous willpower. His thigh brushed against hers as he reached for the beers, handing her one of the glasses.

"To the end of another successful school year," he said, clinking his glass against hers.

She smiled and took a sip. "Do you have any big plans for the summer?" she asked.

"Actually, I'm going to have a little bit longer than the summer off," he replied. "I've requested and been approved to take a sabbatical next year. I've been approached about writing a textbook on creative writing."

"That's wonderful," she said. "God knows you certainly have a talent for teaching the subject. Look at how much you helped me improve."

He took another sip of beer before setting the glass down in front of him. "Yes, but I'm afraid in many ways, you are the exception rather than the rule."

"How so?"

"You, my lovely woman, have a desire to learn, to improve. English isn't even your major and yet you attended every class determined to glean every bit of knowledge and skill I could offer. My success with other students, not unlike your Roy Decker, was considerably less."

"God, please don't ever mention that name to me again. Don't get me wrong. He was a likeable guy, but if I had to read one more paper about him getting wasted or laid, I think I would have thrown myself off a bridge."

Will laughed and she soaked in the sound, aware that she hadn't heard it before. Though he was very free with his smiles, she'd never seen him in the midst of a full-blown laugh. Her heart melted a bit at the sight. He was simply breathtaking.

"I decided several years ago that it's nearly impossible to teach students who don't want to learn. That doesn't mean I don't try, but it's hard for me to stress the importance of writing to nineteen-year-old boys just getting their first taste of true freedom. Sadly, alcohol and girls win nearly every time."

"Nearly every time?" she asked with a grin.

"Okay, you got me. Alcohol and sex win every time. It's one of the reasons why I enjoyed our morning sessions together. You genuinely wanted to learn and I found your enthusiasm and willingness to go the extra mile quite intoxicating."

She acknowledged his compliment with a shy nod, picking up her beer, thinking perhaps a bit of intoxication would make it easier to sit beside him without thinking very naughty thoughts. His gaze sharpened on her face and she wondered again if he could read her mind.

"So," she started, desperately trying to find some way to draw the conversation away from her, "will you go away somewhere to write or stay here in Baltimore?"

"I'll stay here. I'm afraid extensive travel isn't necessary to write this particular textbook, so that wasn't budgeted in. Not that I didn't suggest it," he joked.

"I can't imagine being holed up in an apartment for an entire year just writing." She forced a false shudder, pretending to be horrified.

He shook his head. "I don't intend to drop off the face of the earth. Actually," he looked around the pub, "I like to do my writing around people, in public settings."

Her mind whirled over the idea of Will sitting in this booth, day after day, ordering meals and drinks from her while he wrote. She'd never break free of her obsession at this rate. "You do? I wouldn't be able to concentrate," she said.

"One of the reasons why I dropped by tonight was to check out this special place of yours. Pat's Irish Pub seems like the perfect place to write. Named for your father?"

She nodded. "Yes. Originally, way before I was born, my father only owned this half of the building and the place was just a bar. Then the restaurant next door went out of business and Pop decided to expand."

"I'm assuming the restaurant is through those doors?" he asked, pointing to the left.

"Yes. First thing Pop did when he took over the entire building was cut that opening in the wall," she said. "It's actually a rather large building. This half of the bottom floor is the pub side. People can come in here to have a drink while they wait for their table or just to hang out and watch the game on TV. The restaurant is technically called Pat's Irish

Restaurant, but my mom was the original cook and the locals started calling this Pat's Pub and the restaurant Sunday's Side."

"Sunday?" he asked.

"My mom's name."

"I like that."

"She used to complain about it, but I think deep down, she liked it too. Anyway, the name Sunday's Side stuck. It's not on the sign, but that's what everyone around here calls it."

"And your family lives...?"

"Upstairs."

"I have to admit I'm impressed by the size of the place. I didn't picture such a grandiose old building. I imagine the location doesn't hurt you either."

"Not at all. We have lots of regulars, but we aren't so far off the waterfront that we don't pull in a decent crowd of tourists as well."

He leaned back and placed his arm along the back of the booth behind her. "Your brother is very protective of you."

She glanced toward the bar and watched Tristan glower at her. She laughed lightly as she turned to face Will. "Yes, he is. Actually, all of my brothers are."

"Ah yes, as I recall, you have several."

"Four, to be exact."

Will nodded. "I wonder how your four brothers would react if I leaned over and kissed you right now."

Keira literally felt her heart skip a beat at his comment. Her tongue darted out to moisten her lips, a tiny part of her daring him. "Perhaps you should be more worried about *my* reaction to a kiss."

Where had that flirty comment come from?

He smiled and leaned closer. "I know how you'll react."

She mimicked his movement, inching toward him until

she could feel the breath that accompanied his words. He was going to kiss her. Holy crap, he was going to kiss her. "You do?"

"Mmm-hmm. You're going to go off like a firecracker on the Fourth of July." His lips were so close she could've sworn she felt them brush against hers as he spoke.

"Has anyone ever told you you're arrogant?" she asked.

"Has anyone ever told you you're beautiful?"

She closed her eyes and marveled at the fact they could still be talking when her body was practically shoving her into his lap.

"My mother used to tell me all the time," she whispered. "Monday's child." Her lips rubbed against his as she spoke, but neither of them moved any closer into the kiss.

He placed his hand on her cheek, leaning back just a bit to gaze into her eyes and she wondered why he'd broken away without kissing her. "Is fair of face?" He finished the first line of the familiar nursery rhyme, a question in his voice.

She nodded. "I was born on a Monday."

He pressed his forehead against hers.

"If you don't want this to go any further, Keira, now is the time to say so. I'm interested in pursuing a relationship with you, but I feel I should warn you."

"Warn me?"

"I'm not an easy man to be with."

She pushed away and his hand dropped from her face. She looked at him as the images that had taunted her for weeks drifted through her mind. He'd inhabited her fantasies, turning them down paths she'd never dreamed existed. She blushed as she recalled the recurring vision of him bending her over his desk and spanking her into an orgasm. Had he been sending her signals of his true nature all along? Heaven knew he pushed every hot button in her.

"What do you mean?" she asked.

"Are you familiar with the term *Dominant?*"

"You like to be in charge?" she asked.

"Not the adjective. The noun. I am a Dominant."

"I'm not sure I know exactly what that means," she admitted.

He sighed heavily and pulled away. "I've been battling with my conscience for weeks over approaching you at all, but the fact remains, I'm very attracted to you. Painfully attracted."

"I feel the same. I—" she started, but he shook his head, halting anything else she might say.

"Tell you what. Why don't we just take this a step at a time? I'd love to take you out to dinner tomorrow night. Are you available?"

Actually she wasn't. She was working the dinner shift, but she was fairly certain she could persuade Ewan to trade with her. He was scheduled to wait tables during the lunch rush. "I'd like to go to dinner with you."

He smiled. "Excellent." He glanced over his shoulder at the bar before turning back with a wicked grin. "Now maybe we could test your brother's reaction to this..." He lightly gripped her face, pulling her toward him as his lips descended.

His kiss was exactly what she expected—the perfect illustration of what she'd come to know about him. It was powerful, strong, commanding and she gave herself up to his touch, allowing him to control the moment.

She wasn't sure how long the kiss lasted before a menacing voice sounded from above her. "Want me to freshen up those drinks?" Tristan stood next to the table with his arms crossed against his chest.

Keira and Will broke apart and she giggled at the covert wink he gave her before turning to face her brother. "No thanks, Tristan."

"Yeah well, I thought you were tired, Kiki. Maybe you should call it a night. Go upstairs to bed."

She narrowed her eyes at her brother, prepared to emasculate him for pulling out her cursed nickname in front of Will.

"Kiki?" Will murmured from beside her.

"Don't even think of going there, William Wallace," she threatened.

Will laughed and rose from the table, reaching down to help her up. "Actually, I do need to be going. Why don't we call it a night? Give us both a chance to rest up before our date tomorrow."

"Date?" Tristan asked. "I thought you were working the dinner shift."

"Ewan traded with me," she replied, hoping she could get to her younger brother to make the swap before Tris did.

"I didn't think teachers could date their students," her brother commented, his tone belligerent. He was begging for a fight and Keira couldn't wait until she had him alone to give it to him.

"I'm not Keira's teacher anymore. In fact, I'm on a leave of absence from the college, so I'm not anyone's teacher at the moment." Will's reply was smooth as silk and Keira grinned at her brother, daring him to try to find some other reason to convince them to cancel their date.

"Aren't you a little old to be dating my sister?"

"Tristan Collins!" she said, amazed at her brother's rudeness, but Will cut off her chastisement.

"I'm only thirty-five," he said. "Hardly robbing the cradle. As someone once pointed out to me, eight years isn't so vast a gap."

Now she understood why he'd grinned at her response that first night in his office. Had he been thinking of asking her out even then?

Tristan fell silent and Keira decided to cut him off at the pass before he embarrassed her any further. "I'll walk you out, Will."

He took out a twenty for the beers and started to hand it to Tris, but Keira waved it away.

"The drinks are on me," she said as they headed for the exit.

Once on the sidewalk, they started laughing at the furious expression on her brother's face. "I swear to you, I fully intend to kill him when I go back inside," she assured him.

"Don't do that. He's merely looking out for his sister. I respect the hell out of him for it. Besides," he pushed her back against the wall of the building, caging her in with his arms by her head, "you probably do need protection from me."

"Ah, the Big Bad Wolf, are you?" she teased.

"Yep, and I've come to eat you up." He leaned down and kissed her again, forcing her lips apart to invade her mouth with his questing tongue. She certainly felt as if he could devour her. He'd been driving her crazy for weeks. She ran her fingers through his thick hair, marveling over the softness. She'd dreamed night after night of touching it and now he was here, kissing her. She felt as if she could ride on this cloud forever.

He pulled away far too soon and sighed. "Damn, you tempt me, Miss Collins."

"I think I like the sound of that," she replied.

"There's nothing I'd like more than to keep you out here all night, kissing those lovely lips of yours."

"I definitely like the sound of that," she added, attempting to pull his face down to hers.

He turned at the last minute, giving her only a chaste kiss on the cheek. She frowned, prompting a laugh from him.

"I'll pick you up tomorrow night at seven," he said, pulling away.

She nodded.

"Wear something pretty. I'm going to take you out for a fancy dinner and show you off."

She bristled slightly at his comment before she closed the feeling down.

"Keira, look at me."

She gazed up at his face and saw him studying her intently. "There are many reasons why I'm attracted to you, but your beauty falls rather low down on that list. Don't misunderstand me, I like looking at you, but I *love* talking to you."

Yep, he was definitely a mind reader. "How did you know?"

He grinned. "You shared your feelings regarding outer beauty in a poem you wrote. I understand that you've spent quite a bit of your life feeling as if you have to prove you're more than just a pretty face. Besides, everything you think shows in your eyes."

The damn poem. She really had shared more than she'd realized. Then she considered his last comment and decided in that regard, he was wrong. "No one else seems to have this amazing ESP ability of yours when it comes to reading my mind."

"Perhaps I'm more alert or simply more in tune with you. I'm fascinated by you and that feeling terrifies me just a bit."

"Why?"

"The new, the unknown, can always be a bit frightening."

She could understand that. Her feelings toward him scared the hell out of her and yet, she couldn't resist his pull. He was the force field to her starship and she couldn't wait to be engulfed in his power. She shook her head slightly, trying to dislodge her odd thoughts. She'd be a fool to hand herself over completely to such a formidable man.

His finger touched her cheek gently. "I won't hurt you." She was only confused for a moment until he added with a smile, "Your eyes were speaking again."

"I can see I'm going to have to develop a poker face with you or start wearing sunglasses."

He shook his head. "No, absolutely not. I need to know what you're thinking, what you're feeling if we're ever going to get this relationship off the ground."

"Relationship," she repeated, loving the sound, the idea of that single word.

"Good night, Keira."

"Good night, Will." He kissed her once more, softly, and then he was gone.

⚜

WILL LET HIMSELF INTO HIS APARTMENT AND DROPPED down onto his couch. What the hell was he doing?

He'd convinced himself his fixation on Keira had been based on the forbidden fruit theory. He'd been certain he'd only wanted her because—as his student—he couldn't have her. He'd gone to the pub tonight to prove it to himself so he could move on, move forward, get her out of his head.

One look at the woman had blown that theory out of the water. His attraction tonight—freed from his principles—had elevated to a new high. He'd never felt this way about anyone. He'd never developed an emotional attachment during his affairs, never had a woman call to his heart, his soul. Keira was a sexual innocent and that only made his involvement with her more perilous. She was a vanilla girl and he struggled with the thought of taking her out of her safe, simple world and exposing her to his.

He closed his eyes and leaned his head against the soft cushion. He was exhausted from weeks of agitated sleep and never-ending hand jobs in his shower, attempting to relieve the tension Miss Keira Collins had wrought in his body. He recalled her kisses outside the pub as his tormented cock hardened again. He lightly rubbed the straining flesh through his pants as he remembered her staring at the desk in his office.

It would feel cold against my cheek.

That single comment had played over and over in his head until he thought he would die from the wanting, the needing.

Right or wrong, he feared there would be no turning back now. He wanted Keira, and God help him if she couldn't accept him as he was—because he had the feeling she was the one woman with the power to rip his heart out.

✾   4   ✾

"You look great. Stop fidgeting."

"I look like you," Keira said, tugging on the collar of the gypsy-style shirt she'd borrowed from Teagan. Her shift had run longer than she'd hoped—damn tourist season—and she hadn't had time to go shopping for anything new to wear. Her entire wardrobe consisted of practical pants, jeans and basic tops, so she'd been forced to borrow a skirt and blouse from Teagan. Problem was, her taste and her sister's were as dissimilar as salt and sugar.

"You look great," Teagan reassured again.

Keira glanced down at the wildly colored broomstick skirt and bright purple blouse and considered calling Will to cancel.

"Come on," Teagan said, dragging her away from the mirror. "Let's go wait downstairs in the pub. I can't wait to meet this guy."

"You act like no one ever asks me out."

"Oh, I know guys ask you out, but you never say yes. I've gotta see the one who snagged you," Teagan teased.

She let her younger sister pull her down the stairs and over to the bar. She sighed when she discovered Ewan and Pop helping Tristan mix drinks and Sean bussing the tables at the pub. Teagan was right. She needed to start dating more. Her family was acting like this was frigging prom night.

"I thought you were waiting tables on Sunday's Side," she said to her father and Ewan.

"And miss meeting this guy? Not likely. Joyce and Regina have things under control for now," Ewan replied.

Keira bit back a growl of frustration. "You can't all be standing here like the Spanish Inquisition when he shows up. Just once, do you think you guys could try *not* to embarrass me?"

Tristan wiped up the counter with an evil grin and she knew he was loving that everyone had gathered round. "I don't think there's anything wrong with your family meeting the guy who's taking you out. Isn't that how it was done in the old days, Pop?"

Keira narrowed her eyes, furious with Tris for pulling Pop into this humiliating scene as well. Pop loved to harp on the old ways of doing things and Tristan's pointed question would just get her father fired up.

"It was customary for a man to meet the father. This young man of yours should want to meet me, Keira. It's only polite, after all. Doesn't he have any manners?"

"He's a perfect gentleman, Pop, but I'm twenty-seven. Doesn't that seem a little old for..." She gestured to all of her siblings gathered around.

"Did I miss him yet?" Riley asked, rushing out of the kitchen. "Freaking tourists and their special orders. Is he here?"

Keira sighed and looked at Tristan. "Couldn't get Killian home from Iraq?"

"Not on such short notice," her brother joked, enjoying her discomfiture.

"This is gonna suck," she murmured. "Maybe I'll just wait outside for him."

"We won't embarrass you, Keira. Promise." Sean walked over and grabbed her hand. "We just want to get a look at the guy who was smart enough to ask you out."

Keira grinned and pressed a quick kiss on her baby brother's forehead. "Thanks, squirt."

"Keira?"

She took a deep breath and turned. Will was standing behind her and she tried to ignore that the room had gone suspiciously quiet. There were a lot of regulars drinking at the bar and no doubt Tris had spread the word about his sister having a date. More than a few interested faces turned in their direction.

"Hi, Will."

She saw him glance at her outfit and for a moment, she sensed his surprise. Luckily he recovered quickly. "You look beautiful."

He took her hand as she turned back toward the bar. "Um, I'd like you to meet my family." During his arrival, the men had joined together to form a united front behind the counter. "This is my father, Patrick. Pop, this is William Wallace."

Pop came around the bar and took Will's hand in a firm, quick handshake. "Nice to meet you, Mr. Collins," Will said genially.

"And you. Scottish?"

Will shook his head. "Actually no. My father's side was originally Polish, until Ellis Island Americanized them."

"Polish, eh?" Pop asked.

"Of course, when you throw in my mother's German ancestry, I think it's safe to say I'm a mutt."

Pop laughed and slapped Will on the shoulder. "Well, better a mutt than a Scotsman."

"Pop," Keira warned, trying to steer the conversation back to safer waters.

"These are my brothers," she said, hoping to get this nightmare beginning of a date over with. "You know Tristan. Standing next to him is Ewan and that handsome one on the end is my baby brother Sean."

Will shook all three men's hands.

"And these are my sisters, Teagan and Riley."

"I see beauty runs in the family," he said as he smiled at her sisters. Both of them nodded appreciatively and Riley gave her a thumbs-up and mouthed *he's hot* when Will turned back toward her father.

"I see you're a Ravens fan," Will said, pointing to the endless array of football knickknacks gathered behind the bar.

"Is there any other team worth rooting for?" Pop asked.

Will smiled devilishly and Keira rolled her eyes. "Oh crap, you like football?" she muttered, suspecting Will's next words could easily be his last.

"Didn't I mention I'm originally from Pittsburgh? My parents still live there. Kind of hard to grow up in that city and not be bitten by the bug."

Pop's eyes narrowed. "I should warn you now, William. We don't speak the name of that other team in here."

"Well now, that seems mighty unsporting of you, Mr. Collins. I mean, after all, Super Bowl champions deserve some respect. You gotta admit that record—"

"Luck. It was all dumb luck," Pop insisted.

"Four Super Bowl wins in the last decade is luck?" Will asked.

"Do you hear this?" Pop asked, gesturing at the men seated at the bar, ready to jump into his favorite pastime—arguing about sports.

"Uh, Pop," Keira said quickly. "Will and I really need to get going. I'll let you two bash heads about football another time."

Will smiled and placed an arm around her shoulder. She tried not to show how much his simple, proprietary touch affected her.

"I'll take good care of her, Mr. Collins."

"Ach, what's with this 'Mr. Collins' stuff? We're in the pub. In the pub, I'm Pat."

"It was nice to meet you, Pat, in spite of your misguided loyalty to the Ravens."

Will and Pop laughed and she breathed a sigh of relief. This first meeting had had all the makings of a major disaster, but Will had disarmed them all—well, her Pop and sisters—with his charm. Her brothers were clearly a different story as they remained still as soldiers, throwing threatening glances at Will.

Pop and the girls said their goodbyes and returned to Sunday's Side.

"Well, I guess we'll be going," she said. Then, simply because she owed him, she turned to Tris. "Don't wait up, baby brother."

Tristan scowled at her as Sean walked over to her and Will.

"Be careful," he said with a mischievous grin.

She mimicked his usual reply with a roll of her eyes. "I will. Good night, Sean."

"Ready?" Will asked. She nodded and they left the pub together.

As they walked to his car, she fought to find a way to apologize for her family converging on him on their first damn date.

"You have a terrific family," he said before she could word her apology. "It was nice to meet them all together like that. Now I've got faces for all the names."

"You can't be serious," she said. "That was horrible. Facing a firing squad would have been less intimidating. I'm so sorry they ganged up on you like that."

He opened the passenger door but halted her before she got in. "It wasn't terrible, Keira. You have a lovely family and they clearly love you. I'm an only child and my parents and I aren't close. I enjoyed seeing yours in action."

He bent down and kissed her lightly and as easily as that, her body shifted from first to fourth gear—without stalling.

"I love your kisses," she whispered when they broke apart. He was looking at her intensely, seriously, and she wondered if she'd said something wrong.

"I know this is only our first date, but after spending the last few weeks with you, I feel as if we're much further along," he said.

"I know what you mean," she said. "I can't tell you how glad I am to finally be able to touch you, to kiss you like this."

"How far are you willing to go, Keira?"

She wasn't sure if he meant tonight or in the future, but she realized either way, her answer was the same. "As far as you'll take me."

"God, I hope you mean that," he muttered, and she placed her palm against his cheek to reassure him.

"I do," she said. She suspected from his comments the

previous night that his desires ran a lot darker and deeper than her past lovers', but given the intensity of her fantasies these past few months, she didn't think that would be a problem. They appeared to be standing on common ground in terms of passion.

She got in the car and he crossed around to the driver's side.

"Where are we eating?" she asked as they buckled up.

"It's a little place called Tulley's. It's on the south side and a bit off the beaten track."

"I've never heard of it."

"It's a small place. The owners are friends of mine. I called and told them we were coming. They've assured me they'll save the best table in the house for us."

"Sounds wonderful. Will I meet your friends?"

"Yes, I have a feeling that they'll be anxious to meet you. I don't date often."

"Neither do I," she confessed.

◈

WILL PULLED INTO THE PARKING LOT, TRYING TO CALM THE blood coursing through his body as Keira's words resounded in his brain.

As far as you'll take me.

Dear God. If she only knew the Pandora's box she'd opened with that simple statement. He'd been battling with his conscience since last night and had almost convinced himself that, for their first date, he should keep things simple, safe. He didn't want to frighten her, yet her words had dragged the raging beast within him to the surface and he wasn't sure he could beat it back into submission. Keira, however, may be a different story.

He got out of the car, placing his hands on his hips when she emerged before he reached her door.

"What are you doing?" he asked.

"Getting out. Isn't this the restaurant?"

"I mean you should have waited for me to open your door."

She waved him off with a soft laugh. "I'm the oldest of seven, Will. Believe me, there's very little I can't do for myself."

He didn't share her mirth. "That isn't the point. When you're with me, I'll take care of you."

Her smile dimmed in the face of his seriousness. "I didn't mean to insult you. I'm just used to looking out for myself."

He gave her a grin and walked closer, trapping her between him and the open car door. "That isn't a good enough excuse. After all, I opened your door for you back at the pub. I think perhaps you should be punished for your transgression."

"Punished?" she whispered. He watched her face very closely, fully prepared to back off the moment he sensed she was afraid. His cock went into full alert when her face betrayed not fear, but excitement.

"You were a bad girl and correction is required."

She placed her hand on the car to steady herself and he was treated to a quick glance of her nipples as they tightened beneath her loose-fitting blouse.

"Give me your panties," he commanded.

"What?" she asked.

"I don't ask twice, Keira. Take off your panties and hand them to me. Now."

She glanced around the dark parking lot and he realized her hesitance wasn't based on disbelief, but rather concern at being seen.

"No one can see you. You're perfectly shielded between me and the door. Even if that weren't the case, I would expect you to obey. You have five seconds to comply or I'll add another punishment."

She quickly—and with surprising efficiency—pushed her panties down. She bent slightly to pull them over her shoes before rising to give them to him.

He took them, his chest tightening to discover them damp. "So wet," he murmured, leaning closer to her. She closed her eyes and he knew she expected him to kiss her. He grinned at her sweet innocence. "I'm going to expect a taste of you before the meal is over."

Her eyes flew open. "A taste?"

He lifted her panties to his nose and inhaled. "You smell delicious."

She blushed at his words, watching as he tucked the delicate lace into his sports coat pocket.

"Come. Let's go get something to eat. I'm starving." He gripped her hand and led her to the restaurant. The hostess smiled when she saw him and immediately directed them to the table he'd requested.

In addition to owning the restaurant, his friends, Kent and Jessica, lived a D/s lifestyle. Keira took in the dimly lit, romantic atmosphere as they walked to their table. The restaurant was designed with lovers in mind and most of the tables were filled with couples sitting close, talking quietly.

The hostess took them to a private round table in the corner before returning to her station. Keira started to sit down, but Will stopped her with a hand on her arm. "Pull your skirt up as you sit. I want your bare bottom on that seat."

For just a moment, she looked like she wanted to protest his demand and he wondered if she would balk. Again she took in the surroundings then turned, smiled sweetly at him, and did as he commanded with more grace than he'd ever seen. Jesus. She was a natural submissive.

He quickly took the seat next to her, anxious to hide the truth of her power over him. His cock was threatening to rip through the fabric of his dress slacks.

"I have to admit this feels very strange," she said once they were both seated.

"And yet there you sit. Why?"

"Why?" she asked, no doubt surprised he would question her obedience. "I was hoping you could tell *me* why."

He smiled, reaching over to grasp her hand. "You are an incredible woman, Keira. Trusting, intelligent, lovely. I can't tell you how lucky I feel to be sitting here right now."

"I was sort of thinking the same thing. Not about me," she added quickly, with a laugh, "but about you. You make me feel things, want to do things I've never—"

"Let's not question it yet. Perhaps we could just go with the flow. See where tonight leads."

"I'd like that," she said.

The waiter appeared with a water pitcher and Will grinned as she quickly glanced down to reassure herself the man couldn't see anything. She was perfectly covered from everyone's eyes by the long tablecloth and her position at the table. Her back was to the wall and she was neatly tucked into the corner, hidden from most of the other diners. In fact, there was quite a lot he could do to her at this table that no one in the restaurant would be able to see. The idea of playing with her, touching her as they ate, sent a fresh pulse of arousal through his body.

So much for taking things slow, Will.

He was chomping at the bit to advance their relationship from first-date status to a full-fledged D/s bond. He needed to get control of himself or she'd run screaming from the room.

The waiter finished filling their water glasses and asked if they'd like anything else to drink. "We'll have a bottle of Silver Oak Cabernet. You like red wine, don't you?" he asked, looking toward Keira. He was far too accustomed to ordering for his dates and for a moment, he forgot himself.

"I love it," she confessed.

The waiter smiled and left to retrieve their wine.

"So you come here a lot?" she asked.

He nodded. "As often as possible. As I said, the owners are good friends and the food is delicious. I also like the atmosphere."

She looked around. "The décor is beautiful and it feels as if we have the place to ourselves."

He grinned. "The privacy is one of the things I like best about it." He rested his right hand on the back of her chair, relishing the nearness of their bodies. She leaned closer and he lightly brushed her lips with a delicate kiss. "I believe you promised me a taste of you," he murmured against her mouth.

She moved toward him again but he retreated a few inches. "Not your lips, though they are delicious."

She shivered and he moved his hand from her chair to drape around her shoulders. He wasn't sure if the move was meant to pull her closer or prevent her escape at his next request and he struggled not to consider the act too much. "Run your finger along your pussy. Gather up some of the arousal there and feed it to me."

She looked around the restaurant at the other diners but he cut her perusal short, pulling her gaze to his with his left hand on her cheek. "Don't look at them. Look at me and do what I'm asking."

She pulled in a deep breath and he silently cursed himself

for even starting down this path. What if he'd read her wrong?

She licked her lips, and then, so slowly he thought his heart would burst at the image, she ran her hand under her skirt. He followed her progress with his gaze and his breath caught when she opened her legs. Her damn long skirt prevented him from seeing her touch, but when the pace of her breathing picked up and her eyes began to drift closed he knew she was enjoying the feeling of her own fingers against her flesh.

"Keep your eyes on me," he said. "Are you wet?"

"Yes," she whispered.

"Show me."

Her hand emerged from her skirt and he gripped her wrist to still the shaking of her fingers as she lifted them to his lips. He shook his head at her offer and then, like an artist with a brush, he controlled her hand, painting her lips with her juices before leaning in to lick them clean with a soft kiss.

She sighed as he broke off the kiss, taking her fingers into his mouth to clean them with his tongue. "I don't understand this power you have over me," she whispered.

He jerked back, surprised by her softly spoken statement. "Power?"

"I can't seem to resist the need to do everything you ask of me. I want to give you control. Why?"

She'd asked the question earlier and he'd brushed it aside. Now he felt as if he owed her an answer.

"I can't really tell you why, Keira. I think that's something you'll have to discover for yourself. I suspect it has a bit to do with the fact that you're in charge of every other aspect of your life. You work full-time while attending classes. You care for your family. When do you let go of all of that?"

She shook her head. "My head keeps telling me I'm an independent, adult woman. Am I supposed to let go?"

"Why not? Do you trust me?"

She considered his question and he was glad she was taking the time to figure out her answer. If she'd said yes immediately, he would have doubted her word.

"We haven't known each other that long," she said.

"Is that your answer?" he asked with a grin.

"No...not all of it anyway. My head says I haven't known you long enough to respond to you the way I am."

"Your head would probably be right."

She gave him a quick shrug. "Unfortunately, every other part of me insists I can trust you—that I *do* trust you."

He leaned closer and took her hand in his. "All I can say, Keira, is that I will always be honest with you. Always tell you the truth about what I'm thinking and feeling. The truth about tonight was I'd intended to keep this date very simple, chaste and safe."

She laughed. "You had my panties in your pocket before we even got into the restaurant."

He smiled at her smart-ass comment. Everything about her was open, fun, real.

"I thought I spotted your car in the parking lot," a deep voice said.

Will looked up and saw Kent and Jessica standing at their table, the bottle of wine he'd ordered in Jessica's hands.

"I told the waiter we'd deliver your wine," Kent said.

"I have to admit I'm surprised you've managed to wait so long to make your way over," Will joked. "We've been here ten whole minutes."

Kent laughed. "Jessica's been chomping at the bit to come over and meet your lovely date since you walked in the door."

Jessica elbowed her husband and rolled her eyes. "I was

the one holding *him* back. He's as nosy as an old woman. I'm Jessica Tulley."

"Keira Collins," Will said, taking up the introductions, "I'd like you to meet a couple of my oldest and dearest friends. Kent and I were roommates in college."

"Nice to meet you," Keira said.

"Will says your family is in the restaurant business as well," Kent said.

Keira nodded. "Yes, my family owns and operates Pat's Irish Pub and the adjoining restaurant."

"Sunday's Side?" Jessica asked, and Keira nodded.

"Oh, I've heard wonderful things about that place. Rumor has it you've employed a new chef in the last year."

"My sister, Riley," Keira responded. "She attended culinary school after high school and has just returned to take over the kitchen duties."

"Sister, eh?" Kent said. "Damn. Guess that shoots *that* idea out of the water. We were hoping to lure her away from you."

Keira laughed. "Believe me, there are some days I'd give her to you for free."

"Spoken like a true sister," Kent joked. "Let me give you my card and you can give me a call on one of those days."

Jessica poured the wine as Kent continued speaking to Will. "As soon as Jess heard you were coming, she changed the damn menu. Suspiciously enough, your favorite meal is tonight's special."

Will placed his hand over his heart and smiled. "Ah Jessica, you're too good to me."

"She spoils you," Kent muttered good-naturedly.

Will turned toward Keira. "Is there anything food-wise that you don't like? Any allergies?"

She shook her head. "No allergies, but I can't stand oysters."

Will laughed. "Probably a good thing. I'm not sure you and I would be able to sit for this meal if we added oysters to it."

Keira looked at him, puzzled.

"They're considered to be an aphrodisiac. I'd say we're doing just fine without them."

Her lovely face flushed and her eyes widened at his risqué remark in front of his friends as she smacked him lightly on the arm. "Will," she chastised.

Jessica laughed. "Oh, you'd better get used to that, sweetheart. These two men thrive on teasing."

"And you love it," Kent replied. As he spoke, Will could see Kent's attention spark at Keira's innocent response to his joke.

"Two specials it is then," Will said to Jessica.

"I'll tell the chef to prepare them," she replied.

"That's a lovely necklace," Keira said. "I haven't been able to take my eyes off it. Where did you get it?"

Jessica fingered the choker-style necklace. "It was a wedding gift from Kent," she replied, smiling.

"You have good taste," Keira said to Kent. Will watched his friend nod politely, but he could see the wheels in his best friend's head processing and assessing the situation. Jessica's necklace was a collar, and anyone familiar with the lifestyle would know it. Keira's remark showed her true inexperience.

He'd called Kent this morning to book the table but hadn't mentioned anything in particular about Keira, other than to say he would be bringing a date. His friend had just naturally assumed she would be like all his past dates—older, more sexually experienced, a trained submissive.

"Well, we'll leave you both to your wine. It was nice to meet you, Keira," Jessica said.

"You too."

"Give me a call tomorrow, Will. Maybe we can set up a golf date," Kent added.

Will almost laughed aloud at his friend's lie. Kent couldn't hit a golf ball with a hockey stick. He was facing a serious third degree from his friend in the morning. "I'll do that," he answered smoothly.

As his friends left, he picked up his wineglass. "To us," he said, clinking his glass to hers.

"To us," she repeated.

"I have to admit, Keira, I never noticed this whimsical side of you in class." He gestured to her outfit and she groaned, shaking her head.

"Oh God. I know. Isn't it awful? I almost called to cancel when I realized I had nothing to wear. I borrowed this from Teagan."

He nodded, smiling at her humor. "Ah, well, that makes sense then. I was having trouble reconciling the straitlaced business major to this flower-child-of-the-sixties look."

"I'm afraid my current wardrobe is rather lacking in 'something pretty'," she said, repeating his directions from the previous night. "I'm a jeans girl, through and through."

He considered her comment, wondering how he could verbalize his next thought without pissing her off. "I've noticed that you tend to hide behind your wardrobe. Actually, I've just been sitting here thinking about the way you present yourself in general."

She sobered up at his comment, her posture going stiff in the seat. "What do you mean?"

Oh yeah, he'd definitely crossed into no man's land. "You're a very lovely woman," he said, watching her face carefully. She relaxed a bit until he ruined the compliment with his next words. "You do realize hiding behind ponytails and sloppy clothing isn't going to change that?"

"I don't do that," she insisted.

"I'm afraid you do. You seem to go out of your way to project this image of plainness and I wish you would stop. Give the real Keira a chance to emerge." His words were harsher than he'd intended and when her eyes narrowed, he knew he'd finally gone that one step too far. For all intents and purposes, this was their first date and he was talking to her far too directly, too possessively. "I apologize," he added quickly. "I'm afraid that came out wrong."

"Actually," she said, her voice stiff with anger, "I think it came out exactly right. Last night, when you said you weren't an easy man to be with, that you were a Dominant...is this what you meant?"

He tried to decide how to answer her question. He'd skirted around the details of his private life, sending her far too many mixed signals as he struggled with himself over the correct way to approach her.

He sighed. "This is what I meant."

"If we're to continue dating, you would want to tell me what to wear? What to do?" she asked.

"Not in every aspect of your life, not every minute of the day. Dammit, it's hard to put this into words that won't sound intimidating, threatening."

"Try," she insisted.

"I've come to care about you. I've learned a great deal about you through your writing and our sessions these past few weeks and I want to know more. But I must admit, I tend to suffer from a personality trait that won't let me watch someone I consider a friend harm herself."

"Harm herself? You think I'm hurting myself somehow?" Her voice, though quieter, still held an edge that told him he'd upset her further.

"You work too damn hard. You take far too much onto

your slender shoulders and when you look in the mirror, I'm fairly certain you don't see what the rest of the world does. Keira—you're beautiful. Why hide that?"

"I-I don't know," she said, and he breathed a sigh of relief as he sensed she was calming down. Maybe he hadn't ruined tonight beyond all repair. Yet. "I guess it's just easier than fending off jerks or trying to prove to every person I meet that I'm not stupid."

"Since when does beauty equate to stupidity?" he asked.

"You said you were an only child, right?"

He nodded.

"Well, I'm one of three sisters. Teagan's the talented one, Riley's the outspoken daughter and I'm the pretty one. I don't want to just be pretty."

"I can understand that." He could, too. Keira was a very serious, intelligent woman, but he thought perhaps she was going too far to prove her point. "Maybe, if you'd like, I can help you learn to accept who you are a bit better."

"Give me an example of how," she urged, though he detected a slight trace of wariness in her voice.

"You don't wear makeup, don't style your hair, you wear nondescript clothing all in an attempt to disguise your looks. Keira, you're denying who you are every single day you wake up and walk out of the house like that."

She leaned back against her chair and folded her arms across her chest. He wondered if her body language was her attempt at distancing herself from *him* or from his words. Maybe both.

"I'd like to take you shopping tomorrow," he continued. "Help you pick out some clothing that suits you."

"Suits me or suits *you*?" she asked.

He grinned. "Can't they suit us both?"

The waiter returned with their meals and Will was

grateful for the slight disruption. He was beginning to feel like he was shoving his foot farther in his mouth with every word he spoke.

"I'd like to go shopping with you," she said after several silent moments.

He looked up, surprised.

She wore the most adorable crooked grin and he felt the overwhelming desire to kiss her. "I think I'd like to try on some pretty things and God knows I could use some fashion guidance. It's been a while since I've actually put forth any effort as far as my wardrobe goes."

He smiled at her concession, at her incredibly giving nature. "I'll pick you up at ten."

She laughed and nodded. "As luck would have it, tomorrow is my day off. I'm all yours."

He sucked in a breath at her comment, silently wishing it was true.

$\ast$ *5* $\ast$

As they left the restaurant, Keira struggled to process everything that had happened to her in such a short time. Her feelings for Will were such a jumbled mess in her mind, she wasn't sure which end was up. All she knew for sure was that she wanted him as she'd never wanted another man. With every move he made, every word he uttered, she felt herself falling deeper under his spell.

His comments about her appearance, her clothing, had uncovered a wound she wasn't sure she'd realized had existed until he'd put it into words. As soon as he'd spoken it though, she'd recognized his astute observation as the truth. He seemed to see her, know her better than she knew herself, and perhaps it was that knowledge that drew her to him. He saw her for who she was and genuinely liked her. She felt overwhelmed by the warmth of that feeling and she wanted to revel in its beauty. She'd never known love before, but she sensed that with Will, she could fall fast and hard.

She opened the car door and started to climb in, surprised when Will's strong hand engulfed her upper arm, turning her to face him. One look at his stern face and she realized her mistake.

"Shit," she whispered. "I forgot."

His face was intent and she felt a slight tremor of fear snake through her. "You have two choices," he said. "One, I can take you home, kiss you good night and I'll see you tomorrow morning for our shopping trip."

"What's the second choice?" she asked.

"We go back to my place for coffee."

"I like that choi—"

He cut off her words. "If you return to my place, it is with the knowledge that I'm going to turn you over my knee and spank you for opening that car door. I'm going to take off the kid gloves and give you a glimpse of what you're in for, if you choose to keep dating me."

She shivered at the dark threat and her incredible desire for just such an event. "And if you take me home right now, I get to avoid the punishment? I won't be spanked?"

He grinned. "If you choose to go home now, I'll turn you over my knee in the front seat of the car before we leave this parking lot."

"So I'd get my punishment sooner," she said with a light laugh and he groaned. "I really want to go back to your apartment."

He closed his eyes and pressed his forehead against hers. "God, you're a temptress. I will promise you right here and now, I won't have sex with you tonight."

"What?" she asked, upset by his vow. "Why?"

He kissed her cheek lightly. "Because we're going way too fast as it is and I want you to have time to think about all the things we've discussed tonight."

She realized the intelligence behind his decision, even

though her body was ready to beg him to take her over the hood of his car right now. She forced herself to nod.

"Okay," he said, releasing her arm. "My home it is."

The ride from the restaurant to his apartment was mercifully short. They were both quiet during the drive and she was glad for the few moments of peace to gather her wits about her. She was going to Will's apartment, knowing that he was going to spank her when they arrived.

The thought should appall her, terrify her, but instead she was wetter, hotter, needier than she'd ever been in her life. She squirmed, trying to find relief as Will pulled up to the front of a lovely old house.

"What a nice place," she murmured, hoping the conversation would take her mind off the unbearable pain between her legs. God, one touch and she felt certain she would explode.

"There are only four units in the building. I have half of the top floor."

She nodded and eyed the door handle. Why wasn't he getting out of the car?

"Are you sure you want to come in?" he asked.

Hell's bells. He was giving her an out when all she wanted was to run inside and attack him.

"I'm sure. Please hurry," she whispered, rubbing her legs together once more.

He grinned and shook his head. "Anticipation can make the reward so much sweeter."

"God, Will." She leaned her head back against the car seat, her hand reaching to touch her aching pussy.

"No," he said, quickly grabbing her wrist. "That pussy is mine."

"Then I guess you'd better start taking care of it," she taunted, hoping to push him into action.

His eyes narrowed and she moaned under the power of his

look. "You really are a naughty girl. I was planning on letting you come tonight, but perhaps it would be a more fitting punishment to make you wait."

"I'll behave. Just please, can we go upstairs?"

He made no move to exit the car and, for a moment, she felt an overwhelming desire to scratch his eyes out.

"Open your legs and pull up that silly skirt."

She would have laughed at his distaste for Teagan's clothing if she weren't so thrilled by his command. She slowly pulled her skirt up as her legs drifted as far apart as the car seat would allow. He watched as she bared herself to his gaze and she was amazed by her lack of modesty.

"So beautiful," he murmured as he placed his hand on her thigh, just above her knee.

"Please, Will. Touch me. I'm dying," she insisted.

He chuckled softly. "No, you aren't dying, although the French do refer to an orgasm as *la petite mort*...the little death. Perhaps if I touch you here..."

His fingers moved slowly through the dusting of hair covering her mons, seeking out and finding her clit. He began lightly rubbing the sensitive flesh and her hips instinctively began thrusting forward, in search of more.

"Hold still," he demanded.

"I can't," she said breathlessly. "It feels so good."

"You need to listen and do as I say, Keira. You're only adding to the punishment you're going to receive later."

Who cares?

She placed her hands in his hair, dragging his face forward, wanting his lips on hers. It had been so long since she'd been touched like this. Hell, she'd never been touched like this. His skilled fingers seemed to know exactly where to stroke, how hard, how fast. He moved his thumb to her clit, increasing the pressure as he paused with one finger at the entrance to her pussy.

"Put it in," she begged.

"You aren't allowed to come until I tell you to," he said, slowly sliding the single thick finger inside.

"Oh God," she cried out, relishing the feeling of his thrusting finger and caressing thumb. How could he make her feel like this? His lips caressed her cheek, drifting down to place soft, moist kisses on her neck. She felt the pressure of her orgasm build as he added a second and then a third finger.

"Will, I can't—"

"Not until I say, Keira."

She closed her eyes, throwing her head back, trying to hold off the inevitable. "Can't. Can't," she chanted as he increased his pace, his fingers fucking her hard and deep.

"Can't stop!" she screamed.

"Come," he whispered as she flung herself into the raging inferno, her body trembling with the relief of her orgasm.

She remained still for several moments, trying to assimilate what had just happened to her. Her past experiences with sex had been nothing like that. She was certain she'd never climaxed with such force, with such an intense, glorious impact. It was quite simply the most amazing moment of her life.

Her eyes drifted open and she saw Will smiling at her, his fingers still firmly enclosed inside her.

"Okay?" he asked.

She couldn't express how wonderful she was feeling, so she merely leaned forward and kissed him. When they broke apart, he pulled his fingers from her as she whimpered, the slight movement on her sensitive inner muscles teasing her with yet another orgasm.

"No," he said, covering her legs with her skirt. "No more

of that until we get inside. Damn, watching you come could become an addiction for me."

"I don't mind," she teased as he laughed.

"I'm sure you don't. Let's go in."

❧

AS THEY ENTERED HIS APARTMENT, WILL FORCED HIMSELF to recall the promise he'd made to her in the restaurant parking lot. He'd sworn not to make love to her tonight and, though his body rejected that vow, his mind appreciated the wisdom of it. Over the course of their evening together, he'd come to realize how much he needed this relationship to grow—to last beyond this single night. As a result, he refused to do anything that would negatively impact that outcome.

He shut the door, locking it behind him. "Come on. I'll give you the grand tour. This is the living room," he said, gesturing at the room.

"I love it. I should have known you'd have an eye for color," she said, walking in farther.

"And why is that?" he asked, pleased by her compliment.

"There doesn't seem to be anything you can't do," she said, and he laughed.

"Well, I hate to break it to you, but I can't cook."

"Shit," she murmured. "Neither can I."

"Lucky for us, your family and my friends own restaurants."

"Guess we won't starve," she teased.

He grasped her hand, moving them forward. "There's the kitchen and this is the dining area. There's been a lot of takeout consumed in both of those rooms."

She laughed. "Takeout is good."

"One of the things I liked about this place is that the

entire area is open. And since I don't cook, I generally don't have to worry about the kitchen being a mess." The kitchen was separated from the living room by a long bar, which made the space look larger. He proceeded down the hallway. "There's a bathroom here and at the end of the hall is my master bedroom and another bathroom." Opening a door on the right, he gestured to yet another room. "And this is my home office."

She walked into the spacious room, turning a full circle to take it all in. "And I thought you had a lot of books in your office at school," she said. The entire room was lined with bookshelves, every available space filled with volumes and volumes of books.

"Reading is a guilty pleasure for me."

"Why guilty?" she asked.

"Usually I'm reading when I should be grading papers or preparing a lesson."

"And where does the football fit in?" she joked.

"Every Sunday afternoon in the winter. I'm only human after all."

"You're a male. It seems that, along with a penis, you all share the football gene."

He laughed at her jest, despite the fact that by saying the word *penis*, she seemed to have awakened *his* to her presence. He glanced at his desk and realized she was looking at the same piece of furniture.

So he hadn't imagined it.

"I can take you over my knee or you can bend over the desk." His words were simple and direct and he watched her eyes widen at his abrupt change of subject.

"You're giving me a choice?"

"You will always have a choice in what we do, Keira. I'll never do anything you don't like or that frightens you."

"What if I told you I was scared now?" she asked.

He shook his head and grinned. "You want this as badly as I do. I know the difference between fear and nervous anticipation."

She looked longingly at the desk and he wondered if she'd have the nerve to voice her preference. His alpha male came to the forefront. "Time's up. Go bend over the desk and pull your skirt up to your waist. I want to see your lovely behind, bared and ready for my hand, in ten seconds."

She shivered slightly at his demand before moving toward the desk. He walked behind her and could feel her surprise when she turned to find him standing so close. She walked to the front of the desk and slowly bent forward before reaching behind her to lift her skirt. Unable to stop himself from touching her, he helped her lift the material, dragging his hands along the backs of her thighs.

Once the skirt was around her waist, he lifted her arms, moving them until her hands rested beside her head. "Leave your hands here," he ordered.

She nodded, her head twisted to one side.

"Is the desk cold against your cheek?" he asked, her words from his office at school drifting through his mind.

"Yes," she whispered.

He lightly touched her buttocks and she flinched. He grinned, aware that she was probably suffering from equal amounts fear and desire. It was her first spanking and he was determined to see the job done right. Using his feet, he pressed against her ankles. "Spread your legs apart."

She complied and he was treated to the sight of her juices covering the tops of her thighs. One of the perks of claiming her panties so early in the evening. "So wet," he murmured and she trembled again.

"Why are you being punished?" he asked in a dark voice.

"I opened the car door after you told me not to."

"And?"

"And I was pushy downstairs in the car. Making demands."

Perfect. She was utterly fucking perfect.

He brought his hand down on her buttocks three times in quick succession. While his smacks weren't as hard as he'd used in previous encounters, he wasn't pulling any punches. Her rear end quickly turned a rosy pink and as he continued to pepper her ass with blows, she groaned, thrusting into his smacks, rather than away.

After placing a dozen sharp hits on her rear end, he dragged his hand along her drenched slit, quickly shoving two fingers into her pussy. She cried out and he immediately felt the beginnings of her climax. He pulled his fingers out as she protested.

"Have I given you permission to come?" he asked.

"No sir," she said, her complaints dying on her lips.

He locked his knees at the sound of her voice calling him *sir*, the impact that single word had on him staggering.

He replaced his fingers, driving them into her with more force than he knew he should. She'd shattered his resistance, his will to ease her into the new role. She was born to be his submissive and by God, he wasn't questioning that fact again. She belonged to him and he was about to show her exactly what that meant.

"Will," she cried when he removed his fingers again as she was on the verge of climaxing. "Please, God."

"Not without me, Keira," he commanded. "I own your orgasms. You only take them with my consent."

Her body quivered on the desk as he alternated between the spanking and his fingers fucking her burning-hot pussy.

She was writhing on the desk, her body overheated and

pleading for release. He spanked her ass once more before driving three fingers to the hilt.

"Now, Keira. Come."

She screamed, her body trembling with the power of her climax.

"You're mine," he whispered as her inner muscles pummeled his fingers, squeezing them in the iron-hard grip of her orgasm. "Only mine."

$\mathscr{H}$ *6* $\mathscr{H}$

Keira checked her face once more in the mirror then rolled her eyes at her newfound vanity. She was wearing jeans and a normal blouse, but Will's comments from the previous evening kept drifting back to her. She'd left the top three buttons of the shirt undone, so her tight tank top flashed more than a little bit of her normally well-concealed cleavage. Then she'd taken the time to style her hair, even going so far as to borrow Teagan's curling iron. She'd just put on the last swipe of mascara when Riley had come into the bathroom and let out a wolf-whistle.

"Oh damn. You do have it bad," her sister said.

"What's that supposed to mean?"

"Makeup, fancy hair, fuck-me clothes. You, big sister, have got the major hots for your teacher."

"He's not my teacher anymore and you better not let Pop hear you spouting off the 'F' word or you'll never hear the end of it."

"Where on earth could Mr. Too-Hot-For-Words be taking you so early in the morning?" Riley asked.

"We're going shopping," she replied.

"What?" her sister said, laughing. "You? Shopping? What the hell for?"

"I don't remember you having such filthy language before you headed off to culinary school."

Riley shrugged. "So sue the school. Seriously, what are you shopping for?"

"New clothes," Keira answered. "You saw me the other night in Teagan's outfit. I looked like a clown."

"I didn't think you looked that bad. You just didn't look like yourself."

"Apparently I've never looked like myself."

She thought Riley would question her softly muttered comment, but instead, her sister nodded. "You know, I think you're right. I've never understood why you try so hard to hide your looks. I mean, if I was even half as gorgeous as you, I'd be throwing it all out there, making men drool and women pull their hair out with jealousy."

"You're beautiful, Riley," Keira said, but her sister rolled her eyes.

"Nicely done, Kiki. Way to change the subject from you to me."

"If one more person calls me Kiki this week, I swear to God, I'll kill them. Besides, I don't like to hear you put yourself down."

Riley sighed. "Is Will in favor of you buying a new, hot wardrobe?"

"It was his idea."

"Good. Then buy what he tells you."

Sean yelled down the hall from the living room. "Keira. Will's here."

She snuck one more worried peek at herself in the mirror.

"You'll knock his cock off," Riley assured her, and Keira

laughed as she walked toward the living room. When she arrived, she found Will reading something on a piece of paper and Sean hovering.

"What's that?" she asked.

Will glanced up at her arrival and she sucked in a breath at his appreciative glance.

"You look great," Sean said.

"Thanks, squirt." She gestured at the paper again. "What are you reading?"

"I asked Will to look at my English report. Give me his professional opinion. I suck at English."

"You don't suck," Keira said.

Will spent several moments showing Sean places where he could improve his paper and Keira tried to fight back the pleasure she felt in watching him with her baby brother.

"Ready?" he asked after a few minutes.

She nodded and he held her hand as he led her down through the restaurant and out to the car. "Sean was right," he said as he opened the car door for her. "You look great."

"Thank you," she replied, blushing slightly at his praise.

He got in the car and they talked easily as he drove them to the shops at Hampden. They walked around the quaint streets, stepping into any store that struck their fancy. Will had a wonderful sense of style, choosing several lovely outfits for her to try on. She couldn't wait to go out to dinner with him again so she could wear the little black sheath he'd talked her into buying. It was simple, comfortable and flattered her figure in ways she didn't imagine possible.

She had just taken off her clothing in one shop's dressing room when she heard a soft knock.

"I found another dress I think you should try on," Will said, his voice drifting through the wooden door. The shop was larger than most they'd entered during the day. The employees had been busy at the registers and assisting customers when she'd entered and she hoped to God they still were. She couldn't believe he'd followed her into the women's dressing room. She opened the door a crack to take the dress from him, surprised when he pushed it open and entered.

"What are you doing?" she whispered when he locked the door behind him.

"There's no one else in here," he answered.

"That's hardly the point."

He looked at her in her bra and panties, reaching out to run his fingers along her ribs. "I couldn't stand the thought of you being so close to me and nearly naked. It's been driving me crazy all damn day."

She smiled at his confession—until his next words. He leaned closer, whispering his wishes in her ear. "I want you to get on your knees and suck my cock."

She shivered at the thought of doing such a naughty thing in a public place. She licked her lips, fully aware of how badly she wanted to obey this command, but her sense of right and wrong seemed to be at definite odds. What if they got caught? Could she be arrested for this? What the hell would her father say?

"Now, Keira," he demanded, and she dropped to her knees without another thought. She reached up and unbuttoned his pants. She was about to tackle his zipper when his hands gripped hers. "Use your teeth."

She closed her eyes as a wave of desire rampaged through her. She wondered if it was possible to come from giving a blowjob. If anyone could provoke that response from her, she knew it was Will.

She gripped the tab between her teeth and tugged. It took several moments and a bit of help from Will, but she finally managed to pull the zipper down completely. Keeping one hand on her head, he released his cock with his other and she bit back a small cry at the image of it. Will's cock was thick and long and she couldn't wait to feel it inside her. She pressed her legs together, wishing they were somewhere, anywhere with a bed. Hell, she'd take a furniture store at this point and to hell with the other customers.

He wrapped his fingers in her hair and pulled her forward, directing their play as always. She opened her mouth, taking the head of his cock between her lips and sucking lightly. He groaned softly and she increased the pressure of her pull. His fingers tightened in her hair and she was amazed by how the simple gesture drove her wild. She wrapped her fist around the base of his cock and increased the speed of her sucking. Will gripped her head with both hands, dragging her farther and farther onto his cock. She gagged once at his strong motions and he paused.

She glanced up, surprised to find him studying her face intently. "Take me all the way in, Keira. To the back of your throat. Swallow the head of my cock."

She closed her eyes, panic warring with the desire to follow his instructions. Could she do that and still breathe?

"Trust me," he whispered and she moved forward, engulfing him. She gagged several more times, but sheer determination won out as she finally figured out the timing, swallowing the head of his cock on his next pass.

He moaned and muttered something that sounded like *dear God* and if she'd been able, she would have smiled. She increased the pace as his grip on her hair tightened even more. She sensed he was getting close—and then he said, "Swallow it. Swallow my come."

His cock erupted, hot threads of semen splashing down her throat. She swallowed it all, licking his cock clean, unwilling to give up the joy of bringing him so much pleasure.

For several moments they remained locked in place. She rested her forehead against his stomach as he breathed heavily and she could feel him trying to pull himself together. Finally, his hands reached under her arms and he lifted her.

She whimpered when his leg accidentally brushed between her thighs, touching her clit. She was poised on the edge of a tremendous explosion and she recalled his firecracker comment from the pub. Oh yeah, she was ready to blow. He looked at her flushed face before pushing her back against the wall of the dressing room.

He dragged her panties down roughly and she reveled in his lack of finesse, loving the intensity of his own needs. He lifted her right leg high, the crook of his elbow supporting her under her knee as he held her open.

Voices drifted by the door as two women entered the dressing room. They both held perfectly still, staring at each other silently. The women continued to chatter as they entered other fitting rooms, discussing what they'd found. Keira expected Will to call a halt to their game and was shocked when he captured her lips in a heated kiss at the same time he drove two fingers deep inside her pussy.

She gasped, but he swallowed the sound. Over and over, he drove his fingers into her, dragging her closer to her orgasm. She fought to remain silent, quivered with the effort of not making any noise.

Her climax hovered, yet she knew she couldn't give in. His touch was relentless, hard, wonderful; his kisses endless, deep, passionate. Finally, when she felt certain she would disintegrate from the sheer pleasure, he broke the kiss for only a moment.

Come, he mouthed before returning to her lips. She fell headlong into the climax, her entire body shaking as she returned his kiss, using the motion of her lips on his to express without sound what her voice was dying to scream out.

He held her close to him for several moments as she attempted to regain control of her weakened body. The women in the dressing room left and still he held her.

"I can't believe I let you...that we..." She stopped speaking, unable to find the words.

"You aren't the only one who knows how to be bad. Finish trying on those clothes. I'm going to take you to lunch next and then there's a sex shop around the corner I think we should explore."

"Sex shop?"

"I have a list of toys I want to buy you as long as your leg. So how do you like shopping now?"

"I love it," she replied, giggling. "Can we come again tomorrow?"

"Hurry up." He grinned and slapped her bare ass before exiting the dressing room.

⚜

"I HAD A LOVELY TIME TODAY," KEIRA SAID AS THEY approached the entrance to the pub. They'd shopped all day, spending over an hour in the sex shop Will had suggested. He grinned as he thought about the bag full of toys sitting in his car. He wasn't sure he'd be able to sleep, imagining all the things he wanted to do to Keira's sweet body.

"I wish you didn't have to go." She turned at the doorway to offer him another light kiss. He was making a quick trip home for his mother's sixty-fifth birthday. He'd scheduled the trip months ago and wished he'd known back then about Keira's arrival in his life. Had the timing worked out better he would have asked her to go with him. Unfortunately, she couldn't leave the restaurant short-handed on such late notice and his mother would have a coronary if he sprang a last-minute guest on her.

"I'll only be gone four days," he said, wishing that didn't feel like such an eternity. Leaving Keira was only part of his disgruntlement with the trip. The other part was spending so much time with his parents. He loved them, but they wore him out with their continual health complaints—most based on the fact they were extreme hypochondriacs—and their constant bickering. "I'm driving back Monday morning."

At the crack of dawn.

"Did you leave any clothes in the store?" Tristan asked, coming around the bar to take some of the bags from Keira's hands as they entered the pub. Will grinned and shrugged, his own hands full of their purchases.

"Too hard to decide what to buy. Everything she tried on looked great on her," Will said.

Keira giggled and Tristan rolled his eyes. Will decided perhaps it was time to try to call a truce with her overprotective brother. "She works damn hard. I thought she deserved a treat."

"You bought the clothes?" Tristan asked, anger evident in his tone.

"Some of them," Will replied. "She's too damn stubborn or I would have bought them all."

Keira rolled her eyes. "You're one to talk about stubborn, Will Wallace. I didn't want him to pay for anything," she said to her brother, before looking at Will again and offering the same argument they'd had in the shops. "I'm a grown woman and I earn a paycheck. I can afford to buy my own clothing."

"And as I said, the clothes were a gift."

"You've only been on one date," Tristan added.

Will shrugged. "I've known your sister for months and I

wanted to do something nice for her. Haven't you ever met a woman you wanted to spoil?"

Tristan fell silent and Will glanced at his face. Clearly, Tristan had.

"The last of the original heartbreakers?" Keira asked, laughing, not noticing her brother's silence. "Not likely."

Tristan seemed to recall himself and the sadness Will had seen in his face was quickly replaced with a smirk. "That's me. A regular playboy."

"How are things here?" Keira asked.

"Same shit, different day. Glad you're back, actually. Joyce called in sick and things have been hopping over on Sunday's Side. I know it's your day off, but I'm getting a little worried about Pop. He looks tired."

Will watched Keira's entire disposition switch in an instant. The relaxed nature she'd assumed throughout the day immediately went stiff and alert. "Why didn't you call me?" she asked.

"It's not dire, sis. I'm just saying the old guy could probably use a break right about now."

Will watched as Keira appeared to grit her teeth and he wondered about her sudden anger.

"Sounds like I should leave," he said.

"I really do need to go to work," she said stiffly.

Will was concerned about her swift about-face. He handed the rest of their purchases to Tristan. "Walk outside with me for a minute. I want to say goodbye."

He sensed her desire to refuse him for just a moment. "Keira," he said in a firm voice.

She took a deep breath and nodded her assent, following him back into the late afternoon sunshine.

"Are you okay?" he asked.

"Yeah. I just worry about Pop overdoing it."

He kissed her forehead lightly. "I'm sure he's fine," he said, hoping to soothe her anxiety.

She shrugged. He was sorry to leave her in such a state after the wonderful time they'd had during the day.

"I'll miss you," he whispered, kissing her lightly on the cheek.

The clouds in her face seemed to clear a bit at his admission. "I'll miss you too. You know, I'm afraid you've turned something on inside me that's not going to be so easy to shut down again."

"What's that?" he asked.

"My sex drive."

He laughed. "Oh beauty. I don't want that to shut down. Ever."

"Four whole days," she complained.

"Four days and then you and I are hitting the sheets. You and me and nothing but hours and hours in bed."

"Sounds wonderful."

"Maybe. Maybe not. I'm going to warn you now, Keira. When I get back, you're getting the real deal. The real Will. No-holds-barred. Come Monday, you're mine."

$$\maltese \quad 7 \quad \maltese$$

"Hiya stranger," she said as she met him at the door of his apartment four days later.

"Hiya yourself," he said, grabbing her up and kissing her.

"Mmm," she said after a long, deep kiss. "That kiss almost makes it worth not seeing you for a few days."

"You can have kisses like that anytime you want. Believe me, I'm in no hurry to return to Pittsburgh," Will said as she walked inside and he closed the door behind them.

"How was your mom's birthday party?"

He led her to the couch and they sat together. "Great. Me and the retired folks hanging around a dining room table, eating cake and drinking punch. Do you know how many of my mother's friends have divorced daughters?"

Keira laughed. "Oh man, I'm lucky you made it back at all. I had no idea you'd nearly been sucked into the dreaded bachelor black hole. You should have sent up an SOS or something."

"Yeah, laugh it up. It was a long four days."

She kissed him on the cheek, trying—and failing—to conceal her amusement over his misery. "You're home now. How about I kiss it and make it all better?"

Will's eyebrows wiggled. "I have something you can kiss better."

She rolled her eyes. "I'll just bet you do, but you promised me dinner first. Something smells good," she said, glancing toward the kitchen. "I thought you said you can't cook?"

"I can't. I called Jessica on my way back into town this morning and after she finished laughing hysterically about the fact I invited you to my place for dinner, she took mercy on me and brought by a couple of tonight's specials from the restaurant. Vegetable lasagna and garlic bread."

"Oh yum," Keira replied. "I love veggie lasagna."

"Well. As soon as you take off your clothes, we can eat."

His voice had taken on that edge of command she'd especially missed during his absence and she'd wondered about his vow to show her his true nature upon his return.

"You aren't moving, Keira."

As always, her body reacted to the sound of her name on his lips and she slowly began to unbutton her blouse.

"Aren't you going to get undressed?" she asked when he continued to merely sit and watch her. She pulled off her blouse and dropped it on the coffee table.

"No, I'm not," he replied.

When she paused, he gestured with his hand for her to continue. She stood up and unhooked her skirt, pushing the soft material over her legs. She stood before him in her bra and panties, his silence unnerving her slightly.

"Keep going."

Excitement and sheer curiosity kept her hands moving as she slid her panties down and unhooked her bra. When she was finally naked, she released the pent-up breath she hadn't realized she was holding.

Will threw one of the oversized pillows from the couch on the floor by his feet. "Kneel here. I want to talk to you about something before we eat."

She was grateful for the soft place to land, his command weakening her knees in a way she wouldn't have imagined possible. As she knelt at his feet, he leaned forward and ran his hand through her hair.

"You are truly beautiful."

She blushed, but he shook his head slightly. "I don't mean just your face or your body, but all of you. You have no idea how lovely you are. So tell me," his voice deepened and she shivered slightly at the sound of it, "have you been a good girl?"

She considered his question and nodded. She'd done nothing but work, sleep and eat.

"Did you touch yourself while I was away?"

Her heart increased its pace. "You didn't say I couldn't," she replied quickly.

He frowned at her response. "The night of our first date, Keira. When we were parked out in front of this apartment."

She closed her eyes for a moment as his words drifted back to her.

"What did I say?" he asked. He bent forward, pushing her knees apart with a slight nudge of his toes until she was open to his touch. He ran his fingers through the dark hair covering her mons. "Who does this pussy belong to?"

"You," she whispered.

"Did I give you permission to touch it?"

She shook her head, unable to speak as he teased her clit lightly with one finger. She would never understand how a simple touch could take her breath away, reduce her to a pile of mush.

"Answer me," he demanded.

"No, you didn't give me permission."

"What did you touch it with?" She shrugged, uncertain what he meant until he clarified. "Your fingers? A vibrator? A dildo?"

"My fingers," she confessed.

"Did you come?"

She nodded, aware that her answer would only increase the tension radiating in him. Although she could tell he was displeased, he didn't seem angry and she wasn't afraid.

"How many times?" he asked.

"Just once," she whispered. She shared a room with two sisters and masturbation wasn't an easy thing to pull off. Truth was she'd have played with herself every night if she could have found the time alone. Will had left her in a royal state after their scene in the dressing room and she feared if they didn't have sex soon, she'd be a prime candidate for a rubber room.

"I see." His tone was dismissive and she sensed that the question and answer period was over. What would he do now? She fought against squirming too much, but she was seriously worried about her arousal dripping onto his pillow. She'd never felt so turned-on. She couldn't begin to understand what that said about her, but she honestly couldn't wait to see what his response would be.

"Well, I'd hoped for our first time we'd be able to come together. But it seems you owe me one." He rose as he spoke and took off his tie. "Put your hands behind your back, Keira."

She obeyed, shaking as he tied her hands together at the base of her back. He checked to make sure it was tied tightly enough to prevent escape. "Is it too tight?" he asked. She shook her head as he walked back around to stand in front of her.

"We're going to have to work on this bad habit you have of touching yourself without permission. As long as we're together, your pleasure is my responsibility. I know you have a hard time giving up control, but in this instance, I'm going to insist." He walked away and she watched his retreat to his bedroom.

As she knelt on the cushion, her pussy pleading for attention, she considered his comment. It was one he'd made before. After years of being the responsible one in her family, the one who took care of everything, she wondered if she'd ever be able to truly give herself over to Will.

She'd learned to masturbate quickly and quietly over the years, in an attempt to scratch an itch. Dating was too time-consuming and typically the end results were not worth the effort. Perhaps she'd been looking for the wrong sort of men. Her past dates had been nice, gentle, passive, all too willing to let her decide where they would go and what they would do. After a few years of lackluster sex and boring relationships, she'd simply given up. She couldn't blame her family for converging on Will in the bar the other night. He'd been the first man she'd accepted a date from in over three years.

When he returned, she could see several items in his hands. He smiled and shook his head when he saw her watching him and she wondered what he was thinking.

"What is it?" she asked.

He ran his hand through her hair almost playfully. "I'm afraid you have a lot to learn about being submissive."

She glanced down, studying her posture. She was completely naked with her hands tied behind her back. Her breasts were thrust out as a result and she was kneeling in such a fashion that there wasn't much left to the imagination in terms of her pussy. What the hell more could he want?

"I don't understand."

He placed his hand under her chin and tilted her head back, forcing her to look up at his face. "A good submissive keeps her eyes averted, down toward the floor. She would never look her Master in the eye and never speak unless asked a direct question."

She bit her lip. Master. Is that what she was making him? Master of what? Her life? Her body? Her heart? She didn't know and the thought of giving him so much power wiggled its way into her subconscious, nagging at her before she shuttered the feeling away.

"Amazingly, I have to admit I don't want that from you."

"You don't?" she asked, relief suffusing her.

"Don't get me wrong. I do expect your obedience and as our relationship evolves, I will expect your level of submission to increase, but for right now, this is all new to you. I want you to see what I'm going to do. I want you to feel free to ask questions and voice concerns. I don't ever want you to feel truly threatened by me. Do you understand?"

She nodded.

"Now. Dinner is ready." He knelt in front of her and, as she watched, he showed her the small bullet-shaped vibrator they'd bought together at the sex shop. Dropping to one knee, he quickly slipped the remote controlled device inside her pussy with a grin. "Nice and wet. Damn, I love that about you."

She shared his smile, wondering about the vibrator. She thought he'd intended to punish her, but as he turned the vibrator on, she felt a pleasant hum resonate through her body.

He stood and then reached down to help her rise. Her

movements sent a heavenly jolt through her body and for a moment, she thought she might actually be on the verge of a climax. The vibrator stopped moving.

"Hey," she protested.

He shook his head. "This is a punishment, Keira. Not a reward."

"But—" she started.

He placed his fingers against her lips to silence her. "We're going to sit at the dining room table and eat our lasagna. You're going to fight off the urge to climax, regardless of what that vibrator is doing inside your body. If you make it through the meal without coming, I'll fuck you. If you come before the meal is finished, you'll suck my cock and then I'll take you home. Understood?" He punctuated his question by turning on the vibrator again.

She gasped, a stream of obscenities poised on her lips.

"Think long and hard about your answer, Keira. I could always take you home now."

She bit back her response, her body shaking in the effort to hold off her orgasm. Then she nodded stiffly. "I can't eat with my hands tied behind my back."

"Of course you can. I'm going to feed you."

He led her to the table, helping her sit so her bound hands hung over the low back of the chair. Then he opened her legs, draping her knees over the corners of the seat, leaving her pussy open to his gaze.

He placed a quick kiss on her lips before going into the kitchen to grab their plates. While he was gone, the speed on the vibrator increased and she cried out as it mercilessly tormented her sensitive flesh. She felt a small tear fall down her cheek. She'd never make it.

Dear God, she *had* to make it. The idea of leaving without taking Will into her body was unacceptable. She'd thought of nothing else for four days—four *months* if you counted all the days she'd spent staring at him with unrequited lust as he lectured in his classroom.

"Here we go." He placed the plates on the table and frowned when he spotted the tear on her face. "Are you in pain?"

"I need you," she whispered. Her answer seemed to please him.

"And I need you—desperately, Keira. I know you can do this."

She took a deep breath and nodded, forcing the tears back. He shifted the vibrator back to the lower speed and she sighed with relief.

Her respite was short-lived as Will dragged her through the longest, most erotic meal of her life. He seemed to have grown a third and fourth hand during his absence as he fondled her constantly while feeding her. His hands toyed with her breasts, circling and pinching her nipples until the tiny nubs were larger and more erect than she'd ever seen them. At one point, he rubbed some of his wine into them, bending down to suck the alcohol off. His tongue teased her until she feared she'd broken a bone in her own hand as she clenched them tightly together, fighting off her excruciating need to come.

"God, please," she gasped, aware that her pleading would only lead him to drag out her torture even longer. Through it all, the speed on the vibrator never remained the same, alternating between low, then high, then low again. With every change, her body shook as she fought to adjust, to fight off the orgasm. As soon as she'd weathered one storm, he changed the speed again and she took up the same battle.

He continued to feed her as he played and when she glimpsed the empty plate before her, she tried to remember eating any of it. She couldn't recall the taste of the lasagna or the bread and she was shocked to discover her wineglass was empty too.

When the meal was finally over, Will stood, walking behind her to release her hands. She moaned as they were freed, the pins and needles caused by a lack of circulation making themselves known. He remained behind her, rubbing her shoulders, massaging her arms and her wrists until the slight discomfort disappeared and she felt more relaxed than she believed possible given her current state of arousal.

"I shouldn't have left you bound so long, but you looked so delicious sitting there, I couldn't hold back my gluttony."

"Dinner is over," she said, her voice hoarse from her pleading cries. She'd made it through his torturous, glorious meal.

"So it is," he agreed, helping her stand and turning her in his arms. His embrace was soothing and strong and she melted into him. "You took your punishment very well. I'm proud of you. Who does your pussy belong to?" he asked.

"You," she whispered.

"And your orgasms?"

"They're yours. All yours." She tightened her arms around him.

He reached down and slowly removed the vibrator as her inner muscles instinctually clenched against his fingers. She shivered once more, wondering if the *no climax* restriction was still in place.

"Not yet," he murmured.

"How did you know what I was thinking? My eyes?" she asked ruefully.

"I have to confess, they're more potent than a newborn puppy. I nearly called the dinner to a halt several times. The pleading was almost more than I could bear."

"More than *you* could bear?" she asked, her voice rising. She'd nearly died a million times trying to follow his damn rule and he wanted her to think he'd suffered?

"I've thought of nothing but coming inside that hot body of yours for four days. Believe me, Keira, no one wanted you to pass that test more than I did. Taking you home early would have killed me."

"But you would have done it," she said, aware her words sounded more like a statement than the question she'd intended.

"I would have done it. You have to learn to trust me. A large part of that is proving to you that I'm a man of my word. You can believe what I say to you."

"I..." She paused, then realized the truth of what she was about to say. "I do trust you."

His smile filled his face and she thought he resembled a man who'd just discovered he was heir to a large inheritance. "Come with me," he said, taking her hand and leading her to his bedroom. She'd never seen it before, recalling that her first tour of his apartment had ended with her bent over the desk in his office.

As she entered, she was taken aback by the rich, dark colors and lovely décor. Her first thought was romantic. His bedroom was plush and comfortable and seemed to be decorated with lovers in mind.

"Wow," she whispered as he chuckled.

"I take it you approve?"

"It's so warm, so inviting."

"Jessica helped me decorate it when I first moved in. I have to admit, I had my reservations about giving her free rein, but when I saw the end result, I knew she'd created something special and I've been quite impatient, wanting to share it with someone I cared about."

"You sound as if you've never shown this to anyone."

"I've never brought another woman here," he confessed. Her heart raced at his admission.

"Sometimes I think this isn't real," she said.

He grinned. "Too much, too fast?"

She nodded. "I'm not the kind of woman who does this."

"Does what?" he asked.

"Throws herself into a relationship faster than the speed of light. I've just never felt so much, so soon."

"I don't know if this will help or not, but you aren't alone in that feeling." He took her face in his hands and kissed her as if to accentuate his point. When they broke apart, she giggled.

"What's so funny?" he asked.

"I just realized I've spent the last hour naked, while you're completely dressed. Shouldn't that feel strange?"

He shrugged. "I think it feels just right. But, I agree, I think we'd both be a bit more comfortable right now if I were a little less dressed."

He started to unbutton his shirt but she batted his hands away. "Let me," she insisted, working quickly to divest him of his shirt. When she struggled with the clasp on his pants, it was his turn to take over once more.

After he was completely naked, she forced herself to take a step back. Her gaze drifted to his rock-hard abs and her eyes widened at the sight of his ripped, muscular arms. He clearly lifted weights. His legs were strong and his cock was, well... wow. He was gorgeous.

"I'm not sure I've ever been subjected to such a thorough examination," he teased. "Like what you see?"

She glanced up and saw him regarding her perusal with humor in his eyes. "I love what I see."

"Go get on the bed. I feel the need to fuck you, very badly."

She giggled at his command, walking toward the king-sized bed. The duvet was thick and soft and she admired it as she pulled it down to reveal honest-to-God silk sheets.

She felt Will's cock brush against her spine, his breath hot on her neck. "Crawl in."

He helped her up onto the high bed, following her under the sheets. She wondered how she was stopping herself from jumping on top of him. Her overwhelming need had only grown since dinner and it was taking every ounce of strength in her body to remain calm.

"Lie on your back," he said, positioning her in the center of the bed. He lay beside her, propped on his elbow so—although he wasn't on top of her—she felt covered and wonderfully trapped beneath him.

"I asked you once how far you would go. Do you remember your answer, Keira?"

She nodded. "I said as far as you would take me."

"Give me your hands."

She complied, surprised when he dragged them above her head and secured them to the center of the headboard with restraints she hadn't noticed before.

"I want to touch you," she said, her voice protesting this continued bondage.

He shook his head. "Not this time. There are too many things I want to do to your lovely body and your hands will just be in the way."

"Will," she whispered, the image of him taking her overpowering every other thought in her mind. "I need you."

"Then you'll have me," he assured her. "But first..." He reached into the nightstand drawer and pulled out a long black scarf. He tied it around her eyes and she was plunged into immediate darkness. The sensation only heightened her already powerful arousal and reminded her of his lessons on the senses when they'd worked on her writing.

"Take me into your mouth." She felt him shift on the bed, felt the head of his cock nudge at her lips and she opened them, hungry for the taste of him. This blowjob felt different from her first experience with him in the fitting room. He was rougher, more commanding. His hands engulfed her head as he drove his cock into her mouth. This felt less like a blowjob and more like—

"Your mouth was made to be fucked," he said as he moved in deeply. She savored the feeling of his possession as she took him to the back of her throat, anxious to have his come fill her mouth again.

She cried out when, on one retreat, he pulled all the way out. His lips swallowed her complaints, his tongue thrusting into her mouth, mimicking the movements of his cock just seconds earlier.

She gasped for breath before demanding, "More," when he finally broke the kiss.

"Not this time," he said as he moved down on the bed. His knees bumped into her ass as he nudged her thighs apart and she felt him kneeling between her legs. His lessons in his office on the value of using all her senses were certainly coming in handy now. Without her sight, everything he was doing to her felt stronger, more powerful. His hands spread her legs apart and his hot breath teased the aching flesh of her pussy.

"God," she gasped when his tongue slowly traveled along the slit between her legs before stopping at her clit.

"I didn't get my dessert earlier," he said as he used the tip of his tongue to press down on the sensitive nerves, driving her to the height of madness.

"Have—to—come," she gasped.

"Not until I say so," he said, his voice harsh, commanding.

His tongue returned to her flesh, exploring and taunting every inch of her before entering her. She struggled to breathe as he drove his tongue in and out, fucking her in a way she'd never been fucked before.

She stiffened her body, fighting back her orgasm once more. When he finally allowed her to come, she feared she'd died in the explosion. He read her body almost as easily as he read his damn books, and he pulled out as she was about to hit the pinnacle.

"Damn you!" she screamed.

He chuckled, refusing to rise to her angry bait, and replaced his tongue with two fingers. He shoved them inside without preamble and her back arched in delight as he drove them deeply, roughly.

Three times she climbed to the peak and three times he denied her release. She was quivering, crying, and still he played.

"Please," she whimpered.

"Not yet." His fingers left her pussy despite her body's struggle to hold them inside. He dragged his dripping digits down, pausing at the opening to her anus.

She gasped as he slowly pushed one wet finger inside her ass. "Easy," he murmured, when she tensed up. The feeling, the idea of him invading her ass, felt foreign and yet thoroughly exciting. When his finger was completely lodged inside her tight hole, he paused.

"How far will you go?" he repeated.

His words began to take on a clearer meaning. She lay bound to his bed, blindfolded, his finger buried in her ass, her body screaming for the climax he'd denied for hours—and she understood.

There was nothing he wouldn't take from her. And yet, she knew—really knew—there also wasn't anything he wouldn't give her either.

"Take me," she answered. "Take all of me."

She sensed her words freed something he'd kept restrained, hidden until that moment. He pulled the finger out of her ass, added a second and took her closer to heaven than she'd ever been. He pushed her hard, far, and she reveled in his demands. She heard the tear of foil as he continued to fuck her ass with his fingers. His fist lightly bumped against her clit and she realized he was putting on a condom.

Keeping his fingers lodged in her anus, he pushed the head of his cock into her pussy.

She cried out her relief, her gratitude, her wonder. "Yes," she hissed and he slowly pushed inside, giving her everything she hadn't realized she'd been missing for a lifetime. Once he was buried to the hilt, he paused and placed a soft kiss on her lips.

"Tell me," he demanded. "Tell me what you want."

"Fuck me," she whispered. "Hard."

A second hadn't elapsed before he moved within her. His cock in her pussy and his fingers in her ass drove her to climax in an instant.

"Come," he said and she cried out her release, the inner muscles of her pussy clenching against his relentless cock as he continued to pound inside her. Twice more he led her to the crest, pushing her over into the brilliant white light before he gave in to his own needs.

She moaned when his cock and fingers left her body, relishing the hard, heavy weight of him as he collapsed on top of her. He reached up to release the restraints, removed the blindfold and shoved himself to her side as she took him into her embrace, her kisses mingling with the sweat on his brow.

"Stay the night," he murmured and she grinned at the sleepiness in his voice.

"Okay," she agreed.

"Stay every night."

She leaned back and saw that he had drifted off to sleep, his words beating a tattoo in her brain and on her heart.

Stay every night.

❧ 8 ❧

"Hey Tris. I need two Coronas and a glass of white zinfandel." Keira rubbed her neck, trying to stretch the stiff muscles in her shoulders and back. Since spending the night with Will two days earlier, she hadn't had time to see him again. Pop had suffered another dizzy spell and Keira had confined him to bed, working double shifts and bullying her siblings into doing the same to ensure the man stayed put.

"Busy damn night. You'd think it was the weekend," Tris complained.

"There's a big conference going on. Apparently they let the stockbrokers out for good behavior early tonight." Although the good behavior part was certainly stretching things. She'd slapped away more than a few wandering hands as they'd headed for her ass.

"Here are your drinks," Tris said, handing her the beers and wine. Teagan was singing on the tiny stage in the corner and Keira could see the dark circles under her sister's eyes. Clearly Keira and Ewan were going to have to sit down and study the books, find a way to hire some extra help. Business was doing well and her brothers and sisters deserved to have lives outside the walls of the pub and restaurant. She placed the drinks on the table and turned, running into a solid wall of hard muscle.

"Will," she said, her exhaustion fading away in the face of his welcome company. His eyes narrowed as he studied her face.

"You're tired," he said.

"Look that good, do I?" she teased.

"You look gorgeous, but I don't like these." He ran his hand along the worry lines in her forehead. "Or these," he said as his fingers traced what she was sure were dark circles identical to her sister's.

"Pop still isn't feeling well so the rest of us are filling in."

"Can you take a break?" he asked. "Just a short one?"

She glanced around and caught Ewan's attention. Her younger brother walked over.

"What's up?" he asked.

"Can you cover me for a few minutes?"

Ewan looked Will up and down as she fought to roll her eyes. Her brothers really were going to have to get over these juvenile intimidation tactics. "I guess. But don't be too long. It's nuts in here."

She started to lead Will to a table, but he pulled her up short. "Somewhere private," he whispered in her ear.

She considered his request and led him down a back hallway to a small storage closet. "I'm afraid this is a private as it gets."

"This will do," he said as he closed the door behind him, casting them in darkness.

"There's a light switch behind you," she said, reaching around his large frame to try to find it.

"The dark is fine," he said. "Pull up your skirt and take off your panties."

"Will..." She started to protest, despite her body's immediate willingness to comply.

"Do it now, Keira."

She raised her skirt and started to remove her panties. Will sped the process along and she was surprised by his haste. He was never in a hurry and she actually felt a gush of wetness fill her pussy at the idea of experiencing her first quickie.

"Ooo," she said as she rubbed her hand over his clad cock.

"Careful, Keira. That's not what we're here for," he murmured, removing her hand.

"It's not?"

He brushed a light kiss against her cheek. "It's not," he replied. "Turn around and bend over at the waist. There's a shelf in front of you. Grab hold of it."

She turned, wondering at his odd request until his hands drifted along her ass, then her mind didn't give a shit what he wanted so long as he kept touching her. She gripped the shelf to hold herself steady in the face of his sensual fondling.

"You're working too hard and you're too tense," he said, his hands moving to the slit between her legs. "I thought perhaps I could help you relax."

"Relaxing sounds good," she said, and he chuckled.

"I do love your willingness to play."

She felt a coolness on her ass and she flinched. "Will?"

"Just some lube," he replied. "It'll warm up soon enough."

He worked the slick gel into her ass with one finger as she fought back a groan. Something hard pressed against her anus and she started to rise. His hand on her back held her in place as he continued to push something inside her.

"It's a butt plug," he explained. "It will stretch you so

you're better able to accommodate my cock inside you. It's not as big as I am, but it's a start. Now relax."

She tried to take a deep breath, tried to assimilate to the foreign object he was working into her small opening. When the plug was fully seated, she started to rise but he stopped her again. "Not yet. There's still another hole to fill."

"Another?" she asked as his hand drifted to her drenched pussy.

"I don't want this sweet pussy to feel empty." She felt the vaginal balls they'd purchased together being pushed inside her one at a time, teasing her sensitive flesh as she accepted them.

When he was finished, he reached beneath her and pulled her up. She struggled to stand upright as the toys filled her to brimming. Her breathing, rapid with excitement, hitched at the intensity of being doubly taken by his naughty gifts.

He bent down and bid her to lift first one foot and then the other. She was shocked to realize he was replacing her panties.

"What are you doing?" she asked as he pulled up the scrap of lace and smoothed her skirt back over her hips.

"Helping you relax."

"You don't expect me to wait tables like this?" she asked when she felt him turn around to open the door.

"Of course I do. Don't worry, Keira. I'll be in the pub."

"That's not the point," she protested. "I'm not sure I can walk like this, let alone work—"

"You *can* walk with them inside you and you will," he insisted. "I'll be working on my book and watching over you."

He opened the door and they walked out into the corridor. She sucked in a sharp breath at the balls moving around in her vagina. "Holy shit," she said breathlessly.

He grinned. "I want you to think about how good it's going to feel when I take those toys out and fuck you later."

Her pussy clenched in delight at the thought. "Tonight?"

"I'm going to bend you over that bar once everyone is gone and take you harder than you've ever been taken before."

She shivered at the thought. "Wonder if I can convince Tristan to close early."

Will laughed. "No cheating. It's just after midnight and the bar doesn't close until two a.m. If you're a good girl, I'll give you a little relief around one."

"Damn you," she cursed as she took a couple steps down the hallway before gripping his arm, fighting against the pleasure the toys were causing in her body.

"Breathe deeply and move slowly. You'll be fine."

❦

FOR AN HOUR, WILL WATCHED AS KEIRA WAITED TABLES. He pretended to jot down an outline for his textbook, but in truth he couldn't take his eyes off his lovely girlfriend as she struggled to do her job while fighting back the mother of all orgasms. Her nipples were erect and he'd had to force himself to remain seated as several of the male patrons of the pub ogled her, sexual interest written all over their faces. Perhaps this experiment of his wasn't such a great idea after all.

He'd spoken to her briefly on the phone during the past two days and he could tell she was working too hard and far too worried about her father's health. He'd hoped a little sexual play would take her mind off her troubles and since it didn't seem likely she would come to him, he'd come to her.

If her flushed face and labored breathing were any indication, he'd say he'd achieved his goal. He'd bet a million dollars

Keira wasn't thinking about anything at the moment except the time when he would bend her over the bar and give her exactly what her body was screaming for.

He grinned as she approached him and glanced at his watch. Right on time.

"It's one o'clock," she said, her sultry voice driving even more blood into his already full cock.

"So it is." He rose and gestured for her to sit down in the booth. He'd chosen the same corner booth from the first night he'd asked her out, aware that it provided the seclusion they would need.

Her eyebrows crinkled with confusion and he fought back a laugh. She'd obviously thought he would take her back to the storeroom, but her response to his visit in the dressing room had cued him in to the realization that his lovely Keira wasn't opposed to a little public display of affection.

She sat, hissing as she did so, no doubt pushing the balls in her pussy and the plug in her ass a bit deeper.

He bit back his own groan, his cock throbbing for some sort of relief.

"Put your left leg over my knee," he commanded once they were settled. Her eyes drifted to Tristan and Ewan working behind the bar. "They can't see us," he assured her.

Her leg moved into place, leaving her thighs spread apart enough that he could touch her freely. He wrapped his right arm around her shoulders, drawing her close for a kiss, while his left hand ventured under her skirt.

"What are you going to do?" she whispered when his fingers dipped beneath her panties.

"I want to watch you come."

"Here?" she asked in disbelief, whimpering at the end of her question as he slid one finger inside to play with the balls in her pussy. "Oh God. I can't take this," she said.

She was dripping wet and by the sound of her breathing, he knew it wouldn't take much to bring her off.

"Please, Will," she said as he shushed her.

"Quiet, beauty. Wouldn't want your brothers to hear you. By the way, you can come at will."

"Shit," she muttered, shuddering in the face of his permission.

She closed her eyes and leaned her forehead into his shoulder. He felt her teeth bite into the material of his shirt as he slowly moved his finger inside her, using the balls to rub her G-spot with each thrust. Within seconds, he felt her pussy muscles clench against him, certain she'd bruised his finger with the strength of her orgasm. She was breathing heavily, panting harshly against his chest, her teeth clenched in his shirt. He held her tightly as she trembled in his embrace and he slowly dragged his finger out of her, leaving the balls in place.

"Take them out," she pleaded.

He leaned back to look at her flushed face. "Are you in pain?" he asked, concerned for a moment that he was truly hurting her.

She shook her head. "I don't think I can take much more of this."

He smiled and kissed her gently. "Only one more hour and then I'll fuck you as long and as hard as you wish. You're so amazing," he praised.

He watched her attempt to compose herself before nodding once. "One hour and then you'll do whatever I want."

"Promise," he said.

"GOOD NIGHT," SHE SAID AS SHE WALKED THE LAST customers to the door, locking it behind them. It had been the longest night of her career as a waitress. Will's torturous toys had driven her to distraction with each step she'd taken, but nothing was as crushing to her willpower as Will's close proximity and the knowledge that she couldn't fuck him.

He was currently walking around with Teagan, helping her bus the last few tables. He smiled at her determined look as she approached.

"You look beat, Teagan. Why don't you go on upstairs? I bet I can convince Will to stick around and help clean up," she said, forcing a lightness into her voice she didn't feel. If her sister didn't leave soon, she was going to get one helluva show, because Keira wasn't waiting much longer and she didn't care who stayed to watch.

"I'm not proud," Teagan replied. "You don't have to ask me twice. I'm cooked. Night y'all." Her sister tossed her the dishcloth she was using to wipe up the tables as she headed for the stairs to their apartment. Teagan passed Tristan, who was headed back from the kitchen with the bar glasses he'd just washed.

He sighed tiredly as he placed the rack on the bar and started restocking it with the clean glasses.

"Will volunteered to stick around and help me clean up," she said, certain her sister had been the easy sell. "Why don't you head up to bed, Tris? We can finish this."

Her brother narrowed his eyes at Will and she sensed him struggling to reject her offer just to spite her new boyfriend. However, in her favor seemed to be the reality that Tris really was dog-tired.

She drove the nail in farther. "I'm exhausted myself. Probably won't be more than fifteen or twenty minutes behind you," she lied. Her brother was a champion sleeper. He'd be dead to the world in his bed within five minutes of hitting the top of the stairs.

He shrugged. "Okay. Don't be too long," he warned. She acted annoyed, even though she knew the threat was empty.

Tris left and Keira turned to watch Will lowering the shades on the bar's front windows. He turned off the lights as well so they were left in virtual darkness except for the dimmed streetlights outside that showed through the sheer blinds. The street outside was quiet, peaceful, and it felt as if they were alone in the city.

He walked toward their corner booth and she was surprised by his choice of destination. "Come here," he commanded.

She followed him, the feeling of the toys no less potent than they'd been when he put them inside her two hours earlier. As she stepped up beside him, she was shocked when he roughly turned her toward the booth, bending her over the table. He quickly raised her skirt and pulled down her panties.

"In a hurry?" she teased, though her heart was beating loud enough to drum out any response he may have made.

His fingers dipped inside her wet pussy, pulling out the two balls, one at a time. She looked over her shoulder and watched him place them in the pocket of his jacket before removing it and draping it over the chair of the table behind them. He turned back to face her and opened his pants.

"Have you ever fantasized about being taken by two men at the same time?" he asked.

Red-hot heat flew to her cheeks at his unexpected question.

Holy hell, yeah. Yeah, she had.

"I'll take that lovely blush as a yes," he said, bending over her, caging her beneath his body. The table was hard, uncomfortable against her chest, but she didn't give a damn. The release she'd waited days for was only minutes away from her grasp.

"I-I've thought of it," she whispered when he held still over her. She wondered at his silence after her response.

He shook his head and exhaled a long sigh that warmed her cheek. "Tough," he said. "This is as close as you're going to get to that fantasy. I'll never let another man touch you. I can't." His last two words seemed to be pulled from the depths of his soul and she closed her eyes against the beauty of the feeling that confession stirred inside her.

He rose slowly but she kept her eyes closed, listening as he opened a condom before returning to the opening of her body.

He nudged the head of his cock inside and her eyes flew open at the extreme tightness.

"The plug," she gasped. Surely he didn't mean to take her while the plug was still inside. Suddenly the meaning of his question became clear. "Too much. Too big."

He continued to push inside, stopping often while she attempted to adjust, attempted to catch her breath. For several pleasurably painful minutes, he continued his slow, magnificent glide. Once he was fully seated, he bent forward once more. Every part of her felt filled, consumed, possessed by this wonderful man.

"I promised to give you anything you wanted. You obviously wanted both of your pretty holes filled."

She struggled to understand the tone of his voice. Was he angry, hurt by her fantasy? Surely he knew she only wanted him, only wanted to *be* with him.

"I only want you," she said softly.

Her confession seemed to break the dam of dark, troubling thoughts within him. "Then that's what you'll have."

He stood once more and his cock retreated as he moved away, only to thrust back in fast and hard. She started to scream and he leaned forward and placed his hand over her mouth to block the sound.

He chuckled as he reached above her head for something. A cloth napkin appeared in front of her face. "Open your mouth, beauty. I never thought I'd see the day where I wanted to diminish those lovely screams of yours, but it could be rather awkward if your family came to investigate and found us like this."

She opened her mouth, accepting the gag. The image of her father finding her bent over a table with a butt plug in her ass and Will's cock buried in her pussy was all the convincing she needed to try to hold back her cries.

Over and over he drove into her, holding back nothing. His pelvis rammed the plug in her ass with each return and she felt as if she were being doubly fucked, doubly loved by the amazing man. She came twice, her body trembling violently on the table, the gag in her mouth drenched with saliva and no doubt marred by her teeth marks as she fought, to no avail, to stifle the moans and screams he provoked with each deep thrust.

Her third orgasm built quickly, but the strength of it eclipsed her first two climaxes by far and she heard Will's hushed curse as she pulled him over the edge with her.

"Sweet God," he murmured as her body shook and her pussy clamped on his cock. Her ass throbbed with the sweet, unfamiliar invasion and she shivered as she imagined Will taking her there. She wasn't sure there was anything she'd ever wanted more.

For several moments, Will held himself above her, seemingly reluctant to leave her body. He sighed heavily and stood, his now-soft cock leaving her slowly. She moaned when he pulled the butt plug out and she was surprised how much her body resisted its removal.

"I'm going to leave the plug with you," he said as he reached down to help her stand. Her legs didn't seem capable of supporting her, so he helped her sit on the bench of the booth before refastening his pants and joining her.

"Why?" she asked.

"I want you to start wearing it. Just an hour or so each day. It will stretch you. Get you ready to take my cock there." He studied her face, his brows lowering. "What are you thinking?"

She grinned. "What? You can't tell? I thought you were an expert at reading my expressions."

He shrugged good-naturedly. "You wore me out. I don't appear to be on the top of my game at the moment."

She laughed. "You were too busy being on top of me."

"Minx," he teased and she could see he was still waiting for a response to his question.

She decided to put him out of his misery. "I was wishing you would take my ass right now."

He reared back slightly and groaned. "Crap. Just when I thought my cock couldn't rise to the challenge again."

She glanced down and saw the outline of his erection beginning to form through his pants. She started to reach over to touch it, but he gripped her wrist quickly.

"Not tonight," he said. "Dammit, woman. You don't have an ounce of self-preservation, do you?"

She stuck out her lip in a fake pout. "Please," she said sweetly.

"No," he replied and she could tell by the set of his jaw he wouldn't be swayed. "Your ass has to be sore and I'm not about to hurt you, regardless of the fact it would serve you right for attempting to bite off more than you can chew. Wear the plug a few days and—"

"I'll wear it tomorrow and then tomorrow night, I want your cock in my ass," she demanded.

His eyes narrowed at her haughty reply, but he nodded slowly. An evil gleam lit his eyes and a smile she didn't entirely trust crossed his face. "Have you ever heard the expression *topping from the bottom?*"

She shook her head.

"Yeah, well, I'm going to explain it to you tomorrow night when I have you tied facedown to my bed, spanking your ass."

She disregarded his threatening grin by flashing a mischievous smile of her own. "You'll tell me exactly what I did wrong?" she asked.

He looked at her suspiciously and nodded. "Yes, of course I will. Why?"

She laughed as she answered, "I want to make sure I do it again."

9

Nearly a week had passed since Will's promise to tie her up and spank her, since her demand to experience anal sex. Tris and Ewan came down with the flu and she hadn't done anything except work and take care of two of the biggest male babies God had ever created. She was worn out and sexually frustrated. Will had stopped by nearly every day and had even manned the bar one night, but they hadn't had time to steal more than a few kisses in the back storeroom.

She grinned as she thought about her lovely new boyfriend. *Boyfriend.* It was amazing how such a simple word could make her feel so happy. It had been a month since she'd started meeting with Will each morning in his office for help with her writing assignments, and just over two weeks since their first date. She still couldn't believe how quickly things had progressed, how wonderful everything was between them. She'd always scoffed at the idea of love at first sight, but she had to admit she'd been bitten by some sort of lovebug.

"Aw shit," Riley groaned from behind her.

Keira turned. "What's wrong?"

"You've got that annoying, dreamy look on your face again. God, you are such a putz."

Keira rolled her eyes and smacked Riley's arm lightly with one of the napkins she was folding. "I do not have a dreamy look on my face and I'm not a putz."

"Face it, Kiki. You're falling hard for the college professor. You walk around here with your head in the clouds."

"That's not true."

"I've been standing behind you for two full minutes calling your name."

Keira paused. "Really?"

Riley laughed. "Really. Don't get me wrong. I'm happy for you, sis. I just have to remember to schedule in five extra minutes anytime I want to ask you a question since it takes that damn long to get your attention."

"Sorry," Keira said. "I guess I have been rather distracted."

"No worries. All I wanted to say was I've laid down the law and deemed Tris and Ewan both well enough to come back to work. They're covering the dinner shift. I'm going out and getting drunk tonight if it's the last thing I do."

Keira giggled. "Funny you should mention that. I'd already decided I was going to get laid tonight if it's the last thing I do."

Riley's eyes widened as she grinned. "Careful there, Keira. You're poised very close to the edge of losing your Miss Boring crown and joining the rest of us mortals here on earth."

Keira was used to her siblings teasing her about her calm manner and the fact that, according to them, she didn't have a life. Of course, in a family of emotional, passionate, "Hey everybody, look at me" showboats, it wasn't hard to stick out merely by trying to be the voice of reason, by being reliable.

Besides, someone had to try to keep control of their crazy clan. Her mother had always known how to still the rough waters and Keira had spent the past nine years trying to do the same.

"Okay, I'm off to set up the kitchen staff and then I'm out of here. See you later, sis."

"Have fun tonight, Riley. Be careful."

Riley kept walking and merely waved a hand over her shoulder as she went back to the kitchen.

Keira had just finished setting up the tables for the dinner crowd when Sean walked in from school. He made a beeline for the stairs with his head down. She called out his name, surprised by his odd behavior. She hadn't seen much of her baby brother lately and she felt a twinge of guilt at the realization. In the past, she'd always made time for him, usually as they snuck a bite together for breakfast upstairs or he'd seek her out after school to talk about his day. She tried to recall having a real conversation with him during the past month and she couldn't.

Shit.

"Hey, Sean," she repeated.

"Hey, Keira," he said, not looking back as he headed up the stairs. She stared at the empty doorway, confused by his swift retreat.

She pulled her cell phone out of her pocket and made a quick call to Will, letting him know she'd be coming over tonight. He made a sexy innuendo as she said goodbye and she snapped the phone closed with a grin.

"Who are you talking to, Kiki?" She jumped at the sound of Pop's voice behind her.

"Oh. You scared me, Pop. I was talking to Will," she replied, turning. Unfortunately, her father had taken Tristan and Ewan's flu bug as a calling from God that he was supposed to be working harder than ever. "The boys are better," she said. "They're going to do the dinner shift so it looks like we have the night off." She tried to make it sound as if they were both sharing in the bounty of the unexpected reprieve. Her father was becoming increasingly moody at her continued attempts at making him rest.

"That's good," he said and she thought she detected a twinge of tiredness in his voice. Damn, she was right. He *had* been pushing too hard. "You need a night out with your new young fellow."

She grinned at the thought of Pop considering Will young when her brothers went out of their way to insist he was too old for her. Will had won her father over hook, line and sinker during the past week as he'd continually stepped up to lend a hand around the pub. She wondered what her father would think if he realized her new boyfriend liked the idea of tying her up and spanking her.

"I agree," she said. "Actually, I think I might go upstairs and grab a quick shower. I'll send Ewan and Tris down."

Her father nodded, heading off to the pub. She debated staying behind to check up on him, aware that her father still liked to take a nip of whiskey every afternoon despite the warning attached to his medication. She sighed. She was too tired to fight with him this afternoon and she wasn't so sure the man didn't deserve a drink. It had been a long damn week.

Tris and Ewan were coming down the stairs as she started up. Both just grunted a hello as she passed. The apartment was quiet and she stood in the living room soaking up the peacefulness. With seven people—practically all of them adults—living in the apartment, it was unusual for the place to ever be silent.

She headed for the shower, anxious to wash the grime of the restaurant off, but her conscience nagged at her and she changed direction at the last minute, walking instead to Sean's room. The door was closed and again she was shocked by the strangeness of her brother's behavior. He never closed his door.

She knocked quietly. "Sean?" she called.

It took a few moments for him to answer and rather than open the door as she expected, her merely replied with a, "Yeah?"

"Got a minute? I want to talk to you."

"I'm kinda busy, Keira," he said through the door.

"It won't take long. I just wanted to see how school was going. I haven't had a chance to talk to you much lately."

"School's fine." His answer was short and dismissive. Something was clearly wrong.

"Sean. Open this door. Let me in," she insisted.

She heard him moving around and watched as the door slowly opened.

"Ahh," she said on a quick intake of breath. "Sean, what happened to you?"

Her brother was sporting a dark bruise beneath his eye and a split lip.

He shrugged. "The school tried to call a couple of times, but no one answered. It's nothing, Keira. I just got into a little fight."

"A fight?" She wondered about the school phone call. Ewan had an annoying habit of turning off the phone when he was asleep. No doubt he'd done so today and had forgotten to turn the ringer back on.

Sean looked away from her and her heart broke at the thought of someone hitting her sweet brother. "It's no big deal. You don't need to freak out or anything."

"Don't freak out?" she repeated, aware her voice had increased in volume and pitch. "Who were you fighting with?"

"Chad," he replied.

"Chad? Why? He's your best friend."

"It doesn't matter, Keira. It was just something stupid. Let it go."

"No, I won't let it go. Tell me why you were fighting with Chad."

"No."

"No?" she asked, disbelief rife in her voice. Sean told her everything. She was his confidante. She thought he trusted her.

"Don't you have a date or something?" he asked and she thought she sensed a bit of resentment in his voice. Was that why he wouldn't talk to her? Because of her relationship with Will?

"I do. Later. But I can cancel," she added quickly. "I can stay here. We can hang out."

"I don't wanna hang out, Keira. Go be with Will. That's where you belong."

Dismissed, she left his room and headed for hers. Collapsing on the bed, her mind whirled over Sean's words, the pain she'd seen in his eyes. She should have been here for him these past few weeks. Hell, these past two years. She'd left him to fend for himself. He was finishing high school, on the verge of manhood and she'd deserted him.

Her mind drifted back to her mother. Sunday had been the most patient and giving of mothers. She'd never been too busy to stop whatever she was doing to listen as Keira complained about fights with friends or cried over lost boyfriends. She'd always known she was important to her mother and she'd wanted to offer that same guidance, that same unconditional, limitless love to Sean. She'd failed him.

She'd failed her whole family. Her father's health wasn't improving. Tris seemed more angry and distant by the day.

Killian was in Iraq and she worried about him constantly. She'd left everyone to fend for themselves just so she could get some stupid college degree that probably wouldn't be worth the paper it was printed on once all was said and done. Her place was here. How could she have forgotten that?

Her relationship with Will had blinded her to that fact. She'd been so wrapped up in the newness of being with someone, of exploring so many amazing sexual adventures that she'd lost sight of her responsibilities, of her true calling in life.

Her heart burst as one final, disturbing thought drifted through her mind. She'd let down another person as well. The one person she'd never wanted to disappoint.

Her mother.

❧

WILL SMILED AS HE HEARD KEIRA'S SOFT KNOCK AT THE door. His resolve to keep his hands off her had been weakening with every passing day and he was about to love the socks off Miss Keira Collins. The delightful woman wouldn't know what hit her. He grinned at the thought. He owed her a spanking and he couldn't wait to deliver the delicious, long-overdue punishment.

"You're a sight for sore eyes," he said as he opened the door to his apartment.

She didn't return his smile, instead walking past him quickly without saying a word.

"Keira?" he asked. "Is everything all right?"

She nodded once before freezing and shaking her head instead.

"No," she began. "Not exactly. Will, I've been thinking

lately and I've decided that things between us are moving a bit too fast."

He frowned at her words, trying to make sense of her sudden change of heart. This afternoon on the phone she'd been excited about their plans to, as she'd said, "Fuck their brains out."

"I'm afraid I don't understand," he said.

Her jaw was set and tense and she clenched her hands together so tightly her knuckles were white. Something had upset her. "I just think it would be better if we slowed things down, maybe took a break for a while."

"A break?" he asked, aware of his sharp, angry tone but unable to hold back his alarm. "Keira, what the hell is going on?"

"Dammit, Will! Can't you see, it's too much. Can't you just respect my feelings and let it go at that?"

"No," he said. "I can't. I want—I *need* a better explanation. What's happened to scare you off like this?"

"I'm not afraid," she insisted.

"Yes, I can see that," he replied as his gaze landed on the rapidly beating pulse in her neck and he listened to her strained breathing. She wasn't afraid. She was terrified. But of what? Him?

"The timing on this thing," she waved her hand between them and he felt his fury grow in the face of her refusal to call what they shared a relationship, "is just off."

"Off?" he repeated shortly.

"Things at the pub are crazy. My family needs me right now and I can't keep ditching them to come over here to scratch an itch."

"Scratch an itch?" His voice was dark and if she hadn't been so nervous, she would have sensed the danger in his tone. With each word, she was driving a stake farther into his heart and he worried he wouldn't be able to survive the inevitable fallout of this conversation.

"I don't want you to think I haven't enjoyed our time together, but you have to see, we go too far sometimes. I mean, where is the limit? How far will be too far?"

He stood stock-still as he tried to process her mindset. Too far? She thought their lovemaking needed limits?

"Keira," he said, his voice strained with the effort to speak the words. "I don't think we need to limit our sexuality because we've never done a single thing that was wrong. Why don't you say what you mean? Your problem isn't with the sexual acts, but what they make you feel. Is it the loss of control that's bothering you? The idea of giving up some of that hard-earned power trip you're on?"

She sucked in a breath at his harsh question and he wondered if he'd hit upon the root of her problem or driven her away with his cruelty.

God dammit. She was making him crazy. Making him say terrible things. "Listen, Keira, I didn't mean—" he started, but she interrupted him.

"I don't know what the hell is wrong with everyone! What's wrong with a woman wanting to have a bit of control over her life?"

"Nothing," he said. "But I don't see what's wrong with letting someone else guide the ship every now and again either."

"I can't keep doing this, Will," she said, and he fought to remain impassive to the tears gathering in her eyes. "I can't keep letting my family down."

"Your family? What do they have to do with you and me?"

"They need me. And lately I haven't been there."

"You work in that damn pub from morning to night. You give them everything you can, but Keira, you aren't the mother. It's not your job to raise them. Hell, all of them are already grown."

"I don't think I'm their mother."

"Of course you do and believe me, you use that excuse every time something happens in your life that you can't handle."

"What does that mean?" she asked, her anger suddenly rivaling his.

"You're allowed to have a life too. God dammit, Keira. It's time you grew up and got the hell out of there. Spread your wings. Live a little."

"I'm so fucking sick of everyone telling me I don't have a life! I have a life and I decide how to live it." She was yelling now, taking a step toward him and her fury merely fed his own. "I decide who I want to see, who I want to fuck and you can't tell me otherwise. I don't belong to you."

Her last sentence cut him to the core. "That's where you're wrong," he replied through gritted teeth.

Her eyes narrowed and her nostrils flared. He watched her nipples tauten beneath her tight T-shirt. Jesus, she was magnificent, and she was provoking him like a raging bull with her red flag.

"You want me and you know it. You've belonged to me for weeks—fuck, you've belonged to me since the first day you walked into my class—and there's no way I'm going to let you leave this apartment without a fight."

She took another step toward him, her finger digging into his chest. "Is that right?" she asked. "Well then, Will, I dare you to try to keep me here. I dare you!"

He turned her, pushing her back against the door with more force than he'd intended. He started to release her, started to apologize when she reached up and gripped the lapels of his shirt. With one strong tug, she ripped the material apart, buttons flying as she bent forward and sank her teeth into his chest.

He bellowed from the pleasure-pain of her sharp bite. Without thought to his rushed actions, he pulled her skirt up around her waist and yanked her panties down before shoving her T-shirt over her breasts. He jerked her bra down, releasing her breasts, taking them one at a time into his mouth, alternating between long, hard sucks and sharp bites on each nipple. Her hands hastily unbuttoned his pants, pulling down the zipper and roughly working them over his hips. He kicked them and his boxers off before returning to her breasts.

She held him to her with a painful grip on his hair and he increased the pressure of his suckling until she was screaming and bucking beneath him.

His cock was throbbing painfully but he pulled back. He had to know he wasn't forcing her, wasn't forcing her to do this.

"Keira," he said, her name rumbling through his chest, the sound shattering him like a wrecking ball.

"Don't stop," she demanded, jumping up and wrapping her leg around his waist, trying to pull his cock inside her dripping pussy. "Don't stop. Make me feel so good it hurts."

He lined the head of his cock up and shoved into her in one hard, spine-shaking thrust. She came almost immediately, her nails scraping down his chest, drawing blood. He fucked her as if his life depended on it and for a moment, he considered that perhaps it did. There was no life without her. He pounded into her hot flesh, filling her again and again, the intensity of his blows driving her up the door of her back.

"Harder!" she yelled as she came again.

Still he moved, still he thrust. He hadn't bothered with a condom. She was on the Pill, but he'd never taken her unsheathed. A rush of cum filled his balls as he thought about releasing his semen into her waiting body. That idea triggered the reaction as her next orgasm milked every forceful jet out of him.

She cried out, her hands digging into his forearms, her chest rising and falling with her attempts to take a deep breath. He leaned forward, covering her with soft, pleading kisses, touching every part of her beloved face. A face closed down to him once more.

"Don't do this," he said at last.

"I can't stay," she said, her voice breaking on the words. "I can't keep giving you this power over me." She tried to set herself to rights, pushing him away to pull up her panties, smooth her shirt and skirt back down.

He scoffed at her words. "Don't you see? Don't you get it, Keira? You have *all* the power. Dammit, I'd give you anything you want. Anything. All you have to do is ask."

Tears fell down her face and he realized the mistake of his words the moment he uttered them.

"I want to be left alone." She turned to open the door as she spoke and rushed down the stairs, slamming the downstairs door in her hasty retreat.

❧ 10 ❧

Will shoved his way past Tristan, who appeared to be locking the pub up for the night.

"What the hell do you think you're doing? We're closed," Tristan said, grabbing his arm as he fought to pass.

"I'm not here for a fucking drink. I want to see your sister." Will pushed Tristan back and headed for the stairs to the family apartment.

"Oh no you don't." Tristan grabbed him from behind and Will turned, clenching his fists.

"I'm going up those stairs, Tristan, and I don't care who I have to hurt to get there."

"God dammit, Will!" Tristan yelled. "I'm not stopping you just to be a prick. I'm saying you shouldn't go up there. It's not a good time."

Tristan's words took a bit of the wind out of his sails and he sucked in a painful breath at the thought of Keira telling her family to keep him away from her.

"I just want to talk to her. Apologize," he said, struggling to calm down. He wouldn't do himself or Keira any good if he went upstairs in his current state. It was taking all the strength in his body not to punch something—the wall or her brother top on his list of receivers.

Tristan walked over to the bar and poured a glass of bourbon, pushing it toward him. He followed him to the counter, not sitting down.

"I don't want a drink."

Tristan shrugged. "It's a far cry between want and need, and buddy, if you don't mind me saying so, you look like you *need* a belt."

He picked up the glass, swirling the amber liquid around as Tristan poured himself a shot and drank it.

Will sank down on the barstool miserably, following Tristan's lead and swallowing the alcohol in one gulp, savoring the burn as it glided down his throat. Tristan poured them both another and he guzzled it as well.

"I fucked up," Will said, his voice betraying his misery. Keira's brother probably wasn't the best person to spill his guts to, but the alcohol and exhaustion were taking their toll.

"How?" Tris asked.

Will shook his head dejectedly as all the worries and regrets that had tormented him for two days came bubbling out. "I pushed her too far, too fast. I knew she was an innocent. I was wrong to drag her into my twisted desires like that."

Tristan was silent for several moments, but Will was too consumed with his own depression to consider what the man must possibly think of his confession.

"Keira blames herself for your breakup. Said it was all her fault."

"No," Will insisted. "It was me. I came on too strong. Pushing her into things she wasn't ready for."

"I don't think that's entirely true." Will glanced up, surprised by the man's words. "I don't know exactly what happened between you and my sister and I don't want to know all the gory details—Christ, I *really* don't. I was ready to come by your house today and beat you to a fucking pulp for making my sister cry all night, but Teagan said something this morning that sort of got me thinking. I don't think it's your fault that Keira ran."

"You don't?" Will asked.

Tris shook his head. "When you live with someone, changes come so slow and gradual that it's virtually impossible to see them. I think we all missed something we should have seen a long time ago."

"What's that?"

"Teagan was sort of yelling at Keira, telling her to snap out of it. Teagan's cranky when she hasn't had enough sleep and like I said, Keira's been a bit upset."

Will's heart ached at the thought of Keira crying.

"Don't get me wrong. Teagan wasn't being cruel. She's probably the softest one of the bunch, even if she does come across as someone who never takes things seriously. She told Keira that she needed to start living her own life and stop living Mom's."

Will leaned back as he remembered making the same comment to her the night they fought. She constantly worried about her family. She felt she'd failed them somehow.

"I didn't realize it until Teagan said it. Pop was there and I don't think he'd seen it either, but once I started putting the pieces together, it was just sitting there, as obvious as the sun on a summer day. Bit by bit over the years, Keira put aside parts of herself in her attempt to fill in the gap left in our family when Mom died."

"I know she feels responsible for taking care of you," Will said. "Didn't you all realize that?"

Tris shook his head. "She was eighteen when Mom died. I was fifteen. Like I said, she didn't wake up the day after Mom's funeral and start wearing her clothes. She just sort of gradually started becoming what she thought we needed and the thing that's bugging the hell out of me is...we let her."

Tristan finished his second whiskey, pouring them both a third, and Will could see the man was suffering his own guilt over Keira's apparent meltdown.

"She loves you all. She'd do anything for you," Will said, his words meant to be comforting.

"Even give up her own happiness, her own personality. Shit, Will, this last month with you in her life, she started acting like the old Keira again. I didn't even realize how much she'd changed until my real sister reappeared."

"What the hell am I supposed to do?" Will asked, aware that his chances of making things up to Keira suddenly seemed less likely. He'd mistakenly thought he'd made her run because of his needs, his demands. If she'd run because of some deep-rooted sense of responsibility toward her family, his task had just became insurmountable. He'd never ask her to choose him over her family and he didn't know how to solve the problems she was facing.

"I guess you give her time," Tris answered. "I don't know what you do, Will. Keira's got some seriously fucked-up shit going on in her head right now. I think by bringing the true Keira back out into the light, you triggered some feelings in her that she's gonna have to sort out for herself."

"I was afraid you were going to say that." Will forced a smile. He might not like what Tristan had said, but he appreciated the man's candor. Keira's brother had unwittingly relieved some of the massive amounts of guilt that had been eating away at his gut since Keira ran out.

Tris shrugged and grinned. "Of course, I could be completely wrong. I suck at this bartender shit. People sit on that stool and unload all their problems on me and I never know what the hell to say."

Will laughed. "You did okay tonight."

"Yeah, well, you may not think so later."

"Why's that?" he asked.

"Once all this stuff with Keira blows over, I'm pretty sure I'm gonna have to kick your ass for that 'she was too innocent and I pushed her too hard' comment."

Will threw his hands up in a sign of mock surrender. "Fair enough. I'll consider myself warned. Just so you know though, you throw a punch at me and I'm hitting you back, regardless of the reason."

"I wouldn't have it any other way, bud."

"Guess I'll go home. There doesn't seem to be anything I can do here."

"You driving?"

"No. I only live about two miles away. I think a nice long walk might do me some good. Night, Tristan. Thanks."

"For what's it worth, I hope she figures it out. You don't entirely suck and I actually think you might be pretty good for my sister."

Will laughed. "Thanks for the vote of support."

He walked out into the chilly night air and sighed. He hoped she figured it out soon too because life without her seemed too bleak.

"Well, I expected I might find you here." Pop entered her bedroom and Keira sat up, forcing herself to smile at what she was sure he'd intended as a joke. She'd shut herself in her room the night she'd broken things off with Will. For two days, she'd drifted between sleep and tears, only eating when her sisters forced her to. She'd made a mess of everything.

"I think perhaps it's time you and I had a little talk. A long-overdue talk," Pop began.

Keira sighed, her heart dreading the coming conversation. She'd let them all down. She knew that. She deserved her father's lecture, but she hated knowing she'd disappointed him so.

"Actually," he said, clearing his throat, "I think it's rather a long-overdue apology that's needed."

She fought back the tears that sprang to her eyes. She'd cried so much in the past forty-eight hours she was surprised she wasn't in the hospital suffering from dehydration. She threw her arms around his neck as she spoke. "Oh Pop! I'm so sorry! So sorry. I don't know how I can ever ask you to forgive me. I've been so selfish."

"*You're* sorry?" he asked, pulling away to look at her. "Kiki. *I'm* the one who should be saying he's sorry."

"You?"

"Yes, me. I'm afraid I've let you take far too much on your young shoulders these last few years and I've not realized the pressure you've felt as a result."

"I don't understand." Her father was sorry? She was the one who'd insisted on returning to college when her family needed her. The one who'd started spending all her time with Will and forgetting that her sisters and brothers, that Sean, needed her.

"I think it's time I explained a few things to you. Some things I didn't see until this past month. I—"

She cut him off, certain he didn't understand what she'd done. "Pop, I know that I've been a bit distracted with Will, but you don't have to worry about that anymore. I've broken up with him, so I'll be home more often. I won't let—"

"Keira," her father said sternly. She sucked in a breath at his use of her real name. He only ever used his pet name for her, reserving her real name for times when she'd misbehaved. "You need to stop talking and start listening."

"Okay," she whispered.

"When your mother passed away, I was devastated," he began.

Keira nodded as a tear escaped. She swiped it away quickly.

"I fell apart," he confessed.

"No," she said. She was old enough to remember that time. Her father had been a pillar of strength, keeping the restaurant running, making sure his children had everything they needed.

"Perhaps not externally, not so you could all see, but on the inside, I was shattered. I got up every morning and I went through the motions, but I saw very little. It took me months to pull myself together enough to look around. At that point, you'd graduated from high school. You'd let the fall semester of college come and go without you and you'd assumed responsibility for far more than I should have allowed."

"That's not true," she started, but her father waved her to silence once more.

"You are very much like your mother, Kiki, and I don't just mean in looks, although you are the very spit of her."

She grinned at his familiar expression. She'd often been

confused for her mother by distant acquaintances who hadn't realized her mother had passed away.

"You're like her, but you aren't her."

His voice was strong and sure and she struggled to comprehend what exactly he was saying.

"I don't think I'm her," she said, Will's words drifting back to her.

"You have so many of her personality traits—her strong sense of responsibility, her serious nature, her stubbornness."

"Stubbornness?" she said. "I'm not stubborn."

Her father laughed. "Your mother often swore the same thing, but alas, my dear daughter, you are very, very stubborn."

"How so?" she asked, aware her voice had taken a somewhat haughty tone.

"You assumed your mother's role in this house when you were just eighteen and you've defended that position with the tenacity of a bulldog ever since."

"You all needed me," she protested.

"Yes, we did. We do. But Keira, we need *you*. Not a substitute Sunday."

She closed her eyes against her father's words. "I don't say that to hurt you or to imply that you haven't given this family everything that lovely heart of yours had to share. But I'll be damned if I sit here and let you throw away your own life because of some misplaced notion that we can't exist without you."

"But your blood pressure, your cholesterol—" she began.

"Is pretty much the same as every other mate of mine who's hit sixty years old. I take the medicine the doctor gave me. I eat the rabbit food Riley shovels at me and I've limited myself to one glass of neat whiskey every afternoon—with the doctor's knowledge and permission, I might add."

"Oh."

"Yes, oh."

"I didn't know that," she admitted, suddenly aware that perhaps she did underestimate her father's ability to fend for himself. But her siblings were another story.

"Sean got into a fight at school," she said.

"I know."

"Did he tell you why? What it was about?" she asked.

"He did not."

She sighed, frustrated. "I don't understand why he won't talk to me about it. He used to tell me everything."

Her father chuckled. "He told you everything when he was twelve, Kiki. He's an eighteen-year-old boy, nay, I daresay at this point, he's a man."

She scoffed. "He's still just a boy," she corrected.

"Need I remind you, you were only eighteen when you felt yourself old enough to take over the care of this family."

"That was different."

"How?" he asked.

She sat quietly, unsure of the answer.

"You were an excellent student in high school and I suspect you always regretted giving up your dreams of attending college. Tell me, who was it who convinced you to apply to the university and begin taking classes?"

Keira stared at her father. It was clear his question was hypothetical, but how had he known? "Sean."

"Sean loves you, Keira. He adores you and his heart simply won't let him do or say anything that may hurt you. He's been fighting to find his own way for years, struggling to become his own man."

A pain pierced her heart at the thought of Sean wanting to push her away. "I didn't realize I was annoying him so much."

Her father shook his head, smiling kindly. "Not annoying. Mothering, sheltering, coddling. I feel confident he would have been trying to make the same escape from his mother right now, had she lived."

Keira felt another tear slide, but this time she didn't bother to wipe it away.

"It's time for you to fly away too, Kiki. I've allowed you to stay too long, made you feel trapped—"

"That's not true," she insisted.

"Go. Finish your degree. Be with your Will. Be happy. It's all I've ever wanted for you."

☙❧

Keira stood at the front window of the restaurant, glancing up at the overcast sky. The dreary weather reflected her miserable mood. She'd tossed and turned all night, playing over her father's words and seeing Will's face as she ran out of his apartment.

"What are you still doing here?"

Keira turned to find Teagan standing behind her.

"Go talk to him."

Keira shook her head. "I made a mess of things, Teag. I'm not really sure what I can say to make it better."

Her sister smiled and placed a comforting arm across her shoulders. "You'll say you're sorry and then take off all your clothes. The rest will be easy."

She laughed at her sister's advice before sobering. "I suck at dating."

"That's just because you've only ever tried it with lambs. Will's a lion, king of the jungle. He's not going to be a pushover and he's not going to make things easy, but I have a feeling you wouldn't have it any other way. Besides, it's obvious that he cares about you. One little fight isn't going to change that."

She fell silent as she considered her sister's words.

"Unless you're afraid of lions," Teagan added. "Or happy with things the way they are?"

Keira shook her head. "Not happy. Definitely *un*happy."

"So I'll repeat my previous question. What are you still doing here?"

She hugged Teagan and smiled. "I guess I'm going to see Will."

"I love the decisiveness in your voice. Really inspires confidence in your success."

"Fine. I'm going to Will's and I'm not leaving until he accepts my apology and fucks the hell out of me," she said, her voice louder and filled with glee.

"Whoa, whoa, whoa!" Tris said, coming up behind her. "Damn, I did *not* need to hear that. Shit. I just got a mental image that's gonna cost me a bundle in therapy to recover from."

"Ha ha," Keira said. "I'm going to try to make things right with Will and you, baby brother," she said, tapping him on the chest, "are not going to stop me."

Tris nodded. "You're right. I'm not."

"I'm serious, Tristan, I'm getting sick and tired of this intimidating-brother—" She stopped abruptly. "You're not?"

"Nope." He bent down and shocked her by placing a kiss on her cheek. Tristan was never overtly affectionate. "Will's not such a bad guy and I happen to think he might be pretty good for you."

"You do?" she and Teagan repeated, both of their voices revealing their shock.

He laughed. "I do, but you may want to get out of here and accomplish the deed before I change my mind."

She nodded, hugging her brother tightly. "Thanks, Tris."

He patted her back awkwardly, begrudgingly accepting her

embrace. His uncomfortable response was completely Tristan and she laughed. "Well, here goes nothing."

"Or everything," Teagan added.

"Or everything," she repeated, stepping out into the chilly mid-afternoon air.

WILL STARED AT HIS LAPTOP, THE WHITE PAGE TAUNTING him with its emptiness. He'd sat down on the couch to work on his textbook earlier this afternoon. Three hours later, he still hadn't typed a single word. It had begun to rain, first a sprinkle and now a steady, driving rain that plunged his apartment into darkness. He was too lethargic to even turn on a light.

A soft knock at the door pulled him from his depressed thoughts. It was probably Ms. Davenport from next door. She hated to go out in the rain and was always missing some vital ingredient for a meal or dessert she was making.

He stood tiredly and walked to the door.

"Keira," he said, shocked to find her standing on his doorstep.

"I was in the area," she said. Had he not been feeling so miserable he would have laughed at her clichéd line.

"You're soaking wet."

She nodded and shivered. "I was w-walking here," she began, her teeth chattering.

"You walked? From the pub? In *this* weather?" He dragged her inside, closing the door behind her as they stood on the threshold.

As she spoke, he began to peel her wet things off, grateful when she didn't stop him. She was shivering and he was determined that regardless of her independent nature and their argument, he would take care of her.

"It wasn't r-raining when I l-left. I was h-halfway here when it started, so I j-just kept walking."

He unbuttoned her blouse, dragging the clinging material away from her. "You're drenched. You'll be lucky if you don't catch a cold."

She nodded as he tackled the button and zipper on her jeans. "It was a stupid thing to d-do," she admitted. "I knew it was going to rain."

He peeled the damp denim down her legs as she kicked off her soggy sneakers. Once she was stripped to her undies, he grabbed a blanket from the back of the couch, pulling it around her shaking body.

"What are you doing here?" he asked, aware that his tone was harsher, angrier than he'd intended, but he didn't like the thought of her walking the city streets alone in the rain. Damn woman needed to learn to take better care of herself.

"I..." She paused, leery as she studied his face. He took a deep breath and worked hard to smooth the frustrated lines he was sure she saw there.

"Keira," he said softly, calmer. "Why are you here?"

"I'm sort of new to this relationship thing."

Whatever he was expecting her to say first, that wasn't it.

"I know that," he said, hoping his answer would encourage her to clarify.

"I mean, I've dated in the past, but I don't think my emotions were ever really engaged. I might have thought so at the time, but now I know they weren't."

"How do you know?"

She bit her lower lip and he could almost taste her discomfort, her unease, and he wished he could make this easier on her. She still needed to learn, to comprehend that she could tell him anything.

"Because I feel too much for you. Too much that I don't understand. Too much that I'm not sure what to do with."

"Like what?" he asked.

"When I'm with you, it feels like I sort of change. I can't really explain it."

"Try," he insisted, wrapping his arm around her waist and leading her to the couch. She started to sit but he stopped her, pulling her down onto his lap. The close proximity seemed to ease her a bit as she curled into his chest.

"I've tried to be a good daughter and good sister. For years, I've put my family's needs above my own. Well, no, that's not entirely true. I've put what I *thought* my family needed ahead of my own needs."

"They *needed* you, Keira."

"Oh, I know. Just not in the way I thought they did. I don't think I even realized it for the longest time. You mentioned it the night of our first date when you talked about the way I dressed, the way I hid my true self. When we're together, Will, all of that changes. I sort of become myself again. Only it's not a self I've ever seen before. It's like all the parts I've hidden away for years have decided to come out, only they're magnified a hundredfold. They shine so brightly sometimes, it's blinding and scary as hell. I guess the best way to say it is, you make me feel amazing. You make me feel smart and beautiful and free."

He grinned, pushing her head back so she could look at him as he spoke. "I love how you shine. I've told you before, you're a beautiful woman, inside and out. I never, ever want that light to dim."

She smiled at him before biting her lower lip, her next

words coming hesitantly. "I know what I want now. What I really want," she added.

He remembered her asking to be left alone and, for a moment, a small part of him feared her repeating the request. He nodded, steeling himself for her words. "I told you. I'll give you anything. You just have to ask."

"I want you. Just you."

His smile grew and for the first time in days, he thought he felt his heart begin to beat again. "You already have that, Keira."

Her eyes twinkled at his revelation and she gave him a self-deprecating grin. "I think it only fair to warn you that I'm a complete basket case right now."

"Is that right?" Now that the floodgates had opened, he reveled in the sound of her voice as she unloaded years worth of repressed fears and feelings.

"Oh yeah. My head is moving in about a million different directions. I've lived nearly a third of my life thinking one way and now I've found out I was wrong."

"You weren't wrong," he said quickly.

"I think I understand what you've been saying about loosening up the iron-clad grip I have on being in control all the time."

"You *think* you understand?" he asked with a grin.

"I do understand. I think one of the reasons I'm so incredibly drawn to you is because you help me to let go, cut loose, run wild."

"I like the idea of you running wild."

"Well, that's why I pointed out the fact that I'm new to relationships."

He nodded, recalling her odd opening line tonight.

She continued to explain. "I sort of think there's a good chance I'm gonna screw up this thing between us at least a half dozen more times."

"Just a half dozen?" he asked, teasing her.

"I'll try to limit it to that."

"Well, just be warned that each time you screw it up, I get to take you across my lap and spank your ass until you come." To demonstrate his point, he flipped her quickly, stripping the blanket away and bending her facedown over his legs.

She shivered as he slowing peeled her damp panties over her thighs, dropping them on the floor.

"Did I say half dozen?" she asked, her voice taking on the breathless quality of a woman in the throes of arousal.

"Mmm hmm," he said, rubbing his hand against her bare ass. Her skin was chilly, clammy from her walk in the rain, and he couldn't wait to warm it up.

"I think maybe I should have said a dozen times."

He swatted her ass one time as she spoke.

"Or more like two dozen. I'm pretty green, you know."

He chuckled as he slapped her several more times. She either gave up trying to talk or lost the ability as he spanked her thoroughly, soundly. He'd thought the spanking was for all the worry and pain she'd put him through in the past three days, but as she began to move in time with his hand, he realized this wasn't a punishment at all.

It was a celebration, a reunion, perhaps one of the happiest moments of his life.

He pushed her legs apart, lightly slapping her pussy, his hand slipping slightly in the copious amounts of juices gathered there. She groaned and he repeated the movement, making sure to include her clit on the second and third slaps.

"Will," she cried out as he slipped two fingers inside her hot pussy, driving them in unremittingly, in exactly the way he knew she loved.

"Please," she said.

"Please what, Keira? You only have to ask."

"I want to come and then I want you to fuck my ass."

His hand stilled for a moment, her words ripped straight from his own well-traveled fantasies. "Anything you want."

He added another finger to her pussy and pushed her over the edge, her body shaking, her lovely voice screaming out her release, her pleasure.

His tenuous grip on his own control slipped as he lifted her from his lap and placed her at his feet. "Hands and knees," he commanded and he watched her body quiver at the deep, demanding sound of his voice. He rose and quickly shed his own jeans and boxers, grabbing the bag of sex toys from the end table. He'd pulled them out this morning, tormenting himself with the memories they evoked until he thought he'd go mad.

He knelt behind her. "Open your legs," he said. "I want to get a good look at what you're offering." As he spoke, he retrieved the tube of lubrication from the bag.

She complied and he sucked in a deep breath, fighting to slow down, determined to make this special. Regardless of her past experience, in this she was a virgin and he had to keep that thought in mind.

Then he saw her ass, marked by his hand, and he knew he was fighting a losing battle.

She glanced over her shoulder and he looked up to find her watching him closely. "I'll give you anything you want too," she said, her voice stronger than he'd expected given the strength of her previous climax.

He shuddered at the thought of what she was offering, then shook his head. "I don't think you're ready for what I want. I wouldn't be gentle. I couldn't go slow."

She laughed, a husky, sexy sound that rattled him to the core. "When have I ever asked for gentle or slow?"

He grinned then drifted his hand along her slit before opening the lubrication and applying it liberally to the tight ring of her ass and his cock. "Have you been wearing the plug?"

She shook her head slowly and he realized that for the past three days, she truly had believed their relationship over. It was that thought, that horrible awareness that stirred him to continue. "Well then, this is going to pinch a little, hurt a little, but maybe it will remind you never to doubt us—never to doubt this."

"Fuck me," she said softly. "Make me remember."

He pushed his cock into her pussy twice, using the juices there to coat his flesh as well. She moaned and pushed back toward him. He slapped her ass, hard.

"Don't move," he demanded and he watched her struggle to remain still. "I'm fucking you, Keira. You are to do nothing more than take it. Do you understand?"

"God yes," she hissed. "Do it."

He pulled his cock from her pussy, lining the head up with her anus. Despite his threats, he entered her with caution, slowly, anxious to make sure she could offer what he desperately wanted to take. Inch by inch he forged in, pausing to give her time to adjust. The plug he's used on her hadn't been nearly big enough to prepare her for him. It was a beginner's toy, nothing more, and he'd meant to slowly work her up in size before taking her this way.

As with everything else regarding Keira, nothing ever went as he planned. She'd systematically destroyed his preconceived notions about submission and what he wanted from a woman. She was everything he never knew he wanted and couldn't believe he'd lived a lifetime without.

Seated to the hilt, he stopped, gasping for breath, trying to assimilate to the unforgiving tautness of her ass clenching around him. Christ. It would be a miracle if he could thrust three times without coming.

Keira, until that moment, had held to his command, remaining perfectly still. She turned slowly to look at him and she smiled. Then she turned away from him, lowering from her hands to her elbows and pushing her ass even farther into the air, driving him in just a touch more.

"Fuck me, Will."

Her words released him and he moved out and back in, faster this time. Every thrust increased in speed and force until both of them were crying out from the pleasure-pain of the moment. His climax was long, the come pulled from his balls with the force of a freight train, leaving him to wonder if he'd ever walk again.

"Keira," he whispered as the final drop of semen filled her ass. "God, Keira."

With the last bit of strength left in his arms, he shoved the coffee table away, falling slowly to his side, keeping her back pressed tightly against his chest. He refused to leave the heat of her body and for several moments the two of them simply lay together, connected, side by side.

She broke the silence first. "Will?"

"Mmm," he hummed, unwilling to break the power of the moment.

"I love you," she whispered.

He grinned, placing a soft kiss against her shoulder. "I love you, too."

EPILOGUE

"Okay everybody, they're here. Quiet. Quiet, Riley! Shit, how much of that spiked punch have you had already? Tris, bend down more. I can see the top of your head over the bar," Keira called out across the room.

They'd closed the pub today for a private family celebration. Sean had graduated from high school. They'd all attended the ceremony this morning, sneaking out as soon as it was over to come back to prepare for his surprise party. Pop had stayed behind as Sean gathered up the last of his things and said goodbye to many of the friends he'd grown up with.

Will gripped her tightly from behind, chuckling at her last-minute commands to her unruly bunch of siblings. They were bent down in their corner booth together.

"Shhh," she warned him. He pinched her nipple covertly and struggled to control his cock when a little excited expulsion of breath escaped her lips. Woman was always primed and ready. He should know better than to tease her as he always got taken down in the fall. Then he thought *to hell with it* and grinned as he pinched the other nipple, causing it to peak beneath her T-shirt as well.

"You are the devil," she whispered.

"And you're my angel."

She giggled. "Fallen angel."

"Hush up, you two," Ewan warned from his position beneath a nearby table, "or I'll turn the hose on you."

Pat opened the door, speaking far louder than he needed to. His odd behavior was no doubt making it obvious to Sean that something was up.

"Well, my goodness," Pat practically shouted. "Where is everybody?"

"Surprise!" they all yelled in unison as Keira fought not to roll her eyes. Sean caught their gaze with a less-than surprised but totally pleased look on his face. The black eye had faded and was nearly gone. He still hadn't told anyone what had prompted his fight, but as he and Chad seemed to have made amends, Will had convinced Keira to let it go.

The siblings all gathered around hugging Sean and Will smiled at the image they made. Perhaps one of the most wonderful things Keira had given him this past month was the opportunity to see a large, loving family up close and personal.

Riley snuck into the kitchen and came out with a triple-layer chocolate cake she'd made special for the occasion, claiming it was Sean's favorite. Will dipped out the punch and he made sure to give Sean a cup from the liquor-free punch-bowl when he caught the boy trying to sneak a glass of the spiked stuff.

"Here," Will said, handing Keira a glass. She took a sip and winced.

"How much rum did Riley put in here? I can't even taste the juice."

"There's supposed to be juice in there?" Riley asked with a laugh.

"Christ, the whole lot of us will be falling down drunk if we keep drinking that stuff," she said. "Get some soda, Tris."

"Nope. I sort of like the idea of falling down drunk," her brother replied.

The door to the pub opened and Will did a double take as Tris appeared to have morphed into two people.

"Got room for one more?" the man asked.

"Killian!" The whole lot of Collins siblings yelled their brother's name in unison, every one of them rushing to hug him.

"Sorry about missing the ceremony, Sean," Killian said. "My leave wasn't approved until the last minute and then I had a devil of a time finding a flight. I got here as soon as I could." As he spoke, he walked over and took the glass of punch Will offered. "You must be the professor."

He nodded and took the man's proffered hand. "Yes I am." After spending the past month proving his worth to Keira's other three brothers, he stiffened his spine, prepared to take up the battle once more.

"Nice to meet you," Killian said. "So, Keira, sounds like you finally found a man worthy of you."

Keira shared the surprise he felt at her brother's remark. "Well, I certainly think so," she answered, "but who told you?"

"I did," Tris answered.

"Nay, it was me," Pat replied, "in our phone call Friday night."

"I told you so in that email last week," Teagan added.

They all laughed and Will felt his heart expand at the thought of being included in this amazing family.

"Actually," Will said, placing his hand across Keira's shoulders and pulling her close. "I wanted to..." He paused and looked down at her. She nodded. "We wanted to let you all know that Keira has agreed to move in with me." He looked quickly at her father. "Now I know that's probably not the way you would prefer it, Pat, but..."

Part of their concerns in sharing their plans with the family had been Keira's fear of Pat's response to their decision to "shack up," as she teasingly called it.

"Now son, you don't have to worry about me," Pat replied. "I'm hip to the new ways," he said so stiffly everyone in the room burst into laughter.

"Oh Christ, Pop. What the hell was that?" Riley asked.

"All I'm trying to say is that I think I speak for all of us when I say, welcome to the family, son."

"Hear, hear," Tris said, raising his glass.

The toast was just the first of many as the family lifted their glasses to Sean and to Killian's return, but it was Pat's last toast that meant the most to all of them.

"Raise your glasses one last time," he said. "Here's to the one who couldn't be with us today. She'd be damn proud of every single one of you. You truly are Sunday's children."

Will tightened his grip on Keira as she attempted to covertly wipe away a tear.

"You okay?" he whispered as Riley started handing out plates, telling everyone to eat.

She nodded. "I'm fine."

"I love you, Miss Collins," he said, hoping to lighten the sadness in her face, calling her by the name he'd used in the classroom.

She laughed. "I love you too, Professor William Wallace."

THANKS SO MUCH FOR READING! BE SURE TO CHECK OUT the entire Wild Irish series.
Come Monday
Ruby Tuesday
Waiting for Wednesday
Sweet Thursday
Friday I'm in Love
Saturday Night Special
Any Given Sunday
Wild Irish Christmas

AND DON'T MISS THE NEXT GENERATION, WILDER IRISH.
Wild Passion
Wild Desire
Wild Devotion
Wild at Heart
Wild Temptation
Wild Kisses
Wild Fire
Wild Spirit
Wild Side
Wild Night
Wild Embrace
Wild Dreams
Wild Chance

FANS OF WILD IRISH AND FACEBOOK! THERE'S A GROUP for you. Come join the Wild Irish Facebook group for sneak peaks, cover reveals, contests and more! Join now.

Be sure to join my newsletter for a FREE Wilder Irish short story, One Wild Night.

RUBY TUESDAY

Bad boy rocker Sky Mitchell wants to buy Teagan's song. Only it's not for sale.

Neither is she, but that doesn't stop him from challenging her to a contest, a game of winner take all.

Excerpt:

"Hi again."

Sky looked up to find the singer standing by his table and realized he didn't even know her name. He rose quickly and gestured for her to join him. She placed her glass of water on the table and he nervously decided to take the plunge as they sat down. Perhaps she really didn't recognize him through his disguise, though he feared an introduction would generate the rabid fan response.

"I'm Sky Mitchell," he said.

She never skipped a beat as she replied, "Teagan Collins. Nice to meet you." Her tone gave away nothing and again he was struck by the absurdity of the moment. He'd clearly spent too many years in the limelight if he didn't know how to hold a normal conversation with a new acquaintance.

"Teagan is an unusual name," he said, searching for some scrap to start the conversation since she obviously wasn't going to spend the standard twenty minutes gushing about how great he was and how much she loved his music.

What a relief.

She laughed lightly. "Yeah, well, I have Sunday to thank for that."

"Sunday?"

"My mother. She took the naming of her seven children very seriously."

Sky leaned back in the booth and grinned. "Seven children?"

"Yep." Teagan turned toward the bar. "In fact, if you take a look over there, you'll see two of my four brothers glaring at you from behind the counter."

"Ah, so they are. Should I be preparing for a 'pistols at dawn' challenge?" he joked.

Teagan shook her head, her smile growing wider. "I think you'll be okay so long as you stay on that side of the table. Tris and Ewan have learned a bit about restraint lately. My oldest sister, Keira, just recently moved in with her boyfriend."

"I think I'm beginning to understand your comment about the unusual names—Keira, Tris, Ewan."

"Actually, I have to confess all the names seem to fit. For instance, 'Teagan' means poet."

Sky nodded. "Very fitting for a songwriter."

"Your name is fairly unusual as well," she said.

"It's not my given name," he confessed.

"I didn't think it was. No doubt someone must have

thought Sky was a terribly clever name for the lead singer of a band called The Universe."

"So you *do* know who I am."

"Of course," she said, and then she broke into peals of laughter. He was confused by her response until she added, "Actually, I had no idea until my sister, Riley, spotted you. I mean, I've heard of The Universe, but I have to admit it's not the type of music I usually listen to."

"Not a fan of popular music?" he asked, surprised. While her songs were definitely folksy, "Maybe Tomorrow" would be very easy to put a contemporary twist on by eliminating the acoustic guitar and adding more instruments.

"Not particularly. I prefer folk music. You know, songs where you can actually understand what the singer is saying." The moment the words left her lips, he watched her blush uncomfortably. "I'm sorry," she added quickly. "That was completely rude and I can't believe I said it."

He shrugged good-naturedly. "I'm not offended. I agree there are a lot of bands out there that rely on painfully loud music to drown out the fact that their lead singer can't sing or their words are utterly ridiculous. I hope you don't feel that way about The Universe's music."

She winced. "I was kind of hoping to avoid admitting the fact that I don't really know any of your songs. I mean, it's entirely probable that I've heard them on the radio and just didn't know it was The Universe."

Sky shook his head in disbelief. He wasn't so cocky as to believe everyone in the world knew the band's music, but it had been so long since he'd actually met someone who didn't, he wasn't sure how to react.

He watched Teagan glance at a spot behind him and he realized it was the third time she'd done so. He turned to see what she was looking at. All he saw was a staircase. "Are you waiting for someone?" he asked.

"My sister, Riley. She was excited when she realized you were here. She went upstairs to change her clothes."

He grinned. *That* was a response he could understand. "Is your sister as pretty as you?" he asked.

"She's much prettier. No freckles or bright red hair."

He was surprised by the sincerity of her response, as well as the lack of jealousy behind it.

"Oh Teagan, I had to tell you how much I loved that last song!"

Sky looked up to see an older woman standing by their table. He was struck by the fact that, once again, he was virtually invisible, as the woman never glanced his way.

"Thank you, Mrs. Tibbs."

"Bev wanted me to ask if you were still coming to teach the music class tomorrow."

"Of course I am," Teagan replied. "I wouldn't miss it for the world."

"Music class?" he asked.

Mrs. Tibbs looked at him briefly. "Teagan teaches music at my daughter Bev's preschool every Wednesday."

Sky pictured Teagan surrounded by small children. The thought *lucky kids* drifted through his mind as Mrs. Tibbs turned back to her. "I'm afraid my husband and I are leaving early tonight. His arthritis is bothering him again. Darn cold weather."

"Oh no. Tell him I hope he feels better soon. Good night," Teagan replied.

"Good night, dear." The older woman walked to the front door, where her husband waited to help her into her coat before they left together.

"Apparently Mrs. Tibbs doesn't listen to The Universe

either. I can't begin to tell you what this evening has done for my ego," he joked.

Teagan laughed and he reveled in the genuineness of the sound. After years spent around women who giggled like schoolgirls or offered him husky laughter meant to sound sexy, he enjoyed the true humor behind Teagan's. His cock moved again and he forced himself to think of something other than what she would look like with that ridiculous skirt hitched up around her waist and him kneeling behind her.

"Believe me, Riley will more than make up for Mrs. Tibbs and me. Although I can't understand where she is. Even for her, this is an excessive amount of time spent primping. Maybe I should go check on her."

"Actually," Sky said, taking her hand quickly to keep her from rising. "I was hoping to talk to you about that last song you sang."

"Maybe Tomorrow?" she asked.

He nodded, and then decided to grab the bull by the horns. "It's a terrific song, Teagan. I'd like to record it."

"Record it?"

"I'm in Baltimore for the next month, working on songs I hope to record on my debut solo album." He wasn't sure why he felt compelled to tell her about his plans, but the moment the words flew from his lips, he knew his decision to break away from The Universe was finally made for good. No more waffling back and forth—starting tonight, his new direction was set.

"Solo album? You're leaving The Universe?"

"I'm been toying with the idea for months, but yes," he said more assuredly, "I'm leaving the band." He'd have to break the news to Marty soon, but the fact was his contract with The Universe was about to expire and in a few short weeks, he'd be a free agent. The record company had been hounding him to extend his contract but he'd managed to hedge, claiming personal problems as the hold-up. It was the only time his break-up with Holly had come in handy.

"My song isn't for sale," Teagan said, and the optimistic feeling he'd been enjoying crashed and burned.

"What do you mean it's not for sale? You said yourself you're a songwriter. Isn't it your goal to sell songs?" he asked.

"Yes...no...I mean, I've never really thought about it."

"Never thought about it?"

"I don't write music to make money, Sky. I write songs to make people happy. To share them with my family and friends."

"What kind of Rainbow Brite philosophy is that?" Her lack of drive astounded. Didn't she know how far she could go with her talent?

"'Rainbow Brite philosophy'?" He could tell from her tone he'd pissed her off, but the woman needed a wake-up call. "You pompous ass. There's no reason to insult me. Hasn't anyone ever said no to you before?"

"No one with common sense. I'm offering you a chance to hear one of your songs on the radio, maybe see it hit the *Billboard* list. This could launch your career."

"I have a career," she said.

"Singing in your family's bar in front of a handful of old men. Teaching music to a bunch of kids one day a week. That's your idea of a career?" he asked, uncertain why he was reacting so harshly. For some inane reason, it suddenly felt as if the success of his solo career was inexplicably linked to Teagan's song. Besides, the woman was extremely talented and clearly oblivious to the fact.

"I suppose you think I should be an overly ambitious musician. One who hops on the fast track to fame and fortune with no regard for the quality of my songs, no concern for what junk I produce so long as it makes me rich and famous. Is that right? You know, there are some people out there who actually make music just for the sheer pleasure of it."

Sky took a deep breath, aware that his anger was merely fueling hers. This wasn't the way to negotiate a deal. He knew better than this.

"I'm sorry, Teagan. My reaction was out of line. I've been running on empty for over a year now and I had no right to take it out on you. I love your song. Seriously love it. You said yourself you write songs to make people happy. I'm offering you a much bigger platform to do just that."

She fell silent for a few moments and he could see his words had struck a chord. "Would you change it?" she asked.

He knew this was going to be a sticking point for her, but he refused to lie. He had a definite idea of the sound he wanted and it didn't include an acoustic guitar. "I would add more instruments, change the pacing a bit."

"Electric guitar instead of acoustic?"

"I play the electric guitar."

"You can't play an acoustic one?" she asked.

He sighed and prepared for round two of the battle they seemed destined to wage over her song. "Of course I can, but that's not part of my signature sound. I'm known for my abilities on an electric guitar."

"I don't know how you could make my song mesh with so much noise."

"I hardly consider the music produced from an electric guitar 'noise'," he said, mustering as much patience as he could to keep his tone even.

"Darn it. I did it again. I'm sorry, Sky. I don't think your music is noise. I've never even heard your music. I just don't think you understand the concepts, the subtleties of folk music well enough to do 'Maybe Tomorrow' justice. I would die if my song suddenly sounded like every other song on the radio. Filled with overdone guitar solos, digitally enhanced singing and that blasted repetitive drumbeat. People can't even dance properly to most of the music produced these days. They just bob in place."

"How old are you?" he asked, cursing the words the moment they flew from his lips.

"What's that got to do with anything?" Her eyes narrowed angrily but he couldn't resist finishing his thought. She'd insulted him and his music one time too many—all without even hearing him sing.

"Your ideas about music and dance seem more fitting for a woman in her eighties. Hell, my grandma is more hip about music than you."

"It doesn't have anything to do with being hip. It has to do with personal preferences. If you were educated in more types of music, you'd realize there are some really fine songs out there that don't require more to move you than a single instrument and a beautiful voice."

"You think I'm not educated in music?"

"I didn't say that."

"Yes," he insisted, "you did—and you meant it. For your information, gypsy, I've studied music extensively. In fact, I'll bet I have a better grasp of the subject than you."

She sat up straighter and for a moment, he was finally graced with the shadowy shape of her breasts through her damn loose blouse. Fucking thing was at least two sizes too big in his opinion and he felt his cock stir once again at the sight. Despite her antiquated opinions on music, Teagan had triggered some serious arousal in him. Maybe Marty was right. He did need to get laid.

"Don't do that," she said, leaning closer.

"Do what?"

"Undress me with your eyes."

He grinned. "How about I do it with my hands?"

"Are you finished?" she asked dryly.

"I haven't even started but believe me, when I do, you'll know."

"Can we get back to the conversation at hand?"

"For now. Teagan Collins, I want your song."

"And as I said, Sky Mitchell or whatever your real name is, it's not for sale."

He laughed at her no-nonsense manner. He was enjoying himself, and her casual dismissal of his come-on dispelled his anger and brought out a playfulness he usually only showed to close friends and family.

"Well," he said, "it would appear there's only one way to solve our disagreement."

Ruby Tuesday is AVAILABLE NOW.

ABOUT THE AUTHOR

Virginia native Mari Carr is a New York Times and USA TODAY bestseller of contemporary romance novels. With over two million copies of her books sold, Mari was the winner of the Romance Writers of America's Passionate Plume award for her novella, Erotic Research. She has over a hundred published works, including her popular Wild Irish and Compass books, along with the Trinity Masters/Masters Admiralty series she writes with Lila Dubois.

Find Mari Carr on the web at
www.maricarr.com
mari@maricarr.com

www.ingramcontent.com/pod-product-compliance
Lightning Source LLC
Chambersburg PA
CBHW022008120726
47992CB00001B/471